The Sweetest Thing

By:

Brooke St. James

Other titles available from Brooke St. James:

Another Shot:
(A Modern-Day Ruth and Boaz Story)

When Lightning Strikes

Something of a Storm (All in Good Time #1)
Someone Someday (All in Good Time #2)

Finally My Forever (Meant for Me #1)
Finally My Heart's Desire (Meant for Me #2)
Finally My Happy Ending (Meant for Me #3)

Shot by Cupid's Arrow

Dreams of Us

Meet Me in Myrtle Beach (Hunt Family #1)
Kiss Me in Carolina (Hunt Family #2)
California's Calling (Hunt Family #3)
Back to the Beach (Hunt Family #4)
It's About Time (Hunt Family #5)

Loved Bayou (Martin Family #1)
Dear California (Martin Family #2)
My One Regret (Martin Family #3)
Broken and Beautiful (Martin Family #4)
Back to the Bayou (Martin Family #5)

Almost Christmas

JFK to Dublin (Shower & Shelter Artist Collective #1)
Not Your Average Joe (Shower & Shelter Artist Collective #2)
So Much for Boundaries (Shower & Shelter Artist Collective #3)
Suddenly Starstruck (Shower & Shelter Artist Collective #4)
Love Stung (Shower & Shelter Artist Collective #5)
My American Angel (Shower & Shelter Artist Collective #6)

Summer of '65 (Bishop Family #1)
Jesse's Girl (Bishop Family #2)
Maybe Memphis (Bishop Family #3)
So Happy Together (Bishop Family #4)
My Little Gypsy (Bishop Family #5)
Malibu by Moonlight (Bishop Family #6)
The Harder They Fall (Bishop Family #7)
Come Friday (Bishop Family #8)
Something Lovely (Bishop Family #9)

So This is Love (Miami Stories #1)
All In (Miami Stories #2)
Something Precious (Miami Stories #3)

The Suite Life (The Family Stone #1)
Feels Like Forever (The Family Stone #2)
Treat You Better (The Family Stone #3)
The Sweetheart of Summer Street (The Family Stone #4)
Out of Nowhere (The Family Stone #5)

Delicate Balance (The Blair Brothers #1)
Cherished (The Blair Brothers #2)
The Whole Story (The Blair Brothers #3)
Dream Chaser (Blair Brothers #4)

Kiss & Tell (Novella) (Tanner Family #0)
Mischief & Mayhem (Tanner Family #1
Reckless & Wild (Tanner Family #2)
Heart & Soul (Tanner Family #3)
Me & Mister Everything (Tanner Family #4)
Through & Through (Tanner Family #5)
Lost & Found (Tanner Family #6)
Sparks & Embers (Tanner Family #7)
Young & Wild (Tanner Family #8)

Easy Does It (Bank Street Stories #1)
The Trouble with Crushes (Bank Street Stories #2)
A King for Christmas (Novella) (A Bank Street Christmas)
Diamonds Are Forever (Bank Street Stories #3)
Secret Rooms and Stolen Kisses (Bank Street Stories #4)
Feels Like Home (Bank Street Stories #5)
Just Like Romeo and Juliet (Bank Street Stories #6)
See You in Seattle (Bank Street Stories #7)
The Sweetest Thing (Bank Street Stories #8)

4

Chapter 1

January
Seattle, Washington

Katie Klein, daughter of Drew and Lucy Klein, granddaughter of Daniel and Abby King.

I was a middle child. I had heard, several times in my life, that there was some sort of stigma with that, but it never felt that way to me. Maybe it was because I was the only girl with an older and younger brother. Either way, I never felt like I got the short end of any stick where my birth order was concerned.

I didn't get many short ends of sticks at all, to be honest. I grew up with multiple famous people in my family. I got to go to nice schools and attend cool events. My dad worked as a judge in Galveston where basically all of my mom's family lived. My mom was a well-known author who recently wrote a young adult series that got made into a major movie. My great uncle was a famous boxer named Billy Castro, and my aunt, Billy's wife, was a successful painter. My grandfather on my dad's side was a senator. We had ties in Houston where I spent my early childhood, and in Galveston where most of my family was currently. My aunts and uncles and other extended family had businesses in Galveston, and we knew everyone there.

Even at twenty-six, I was still reaping the benefits of my generous family. I currently lived in Seattle, Washington with my older brother, Mac. He bought a mansion, and two of our cousins, Ozzy and Bri, moved up there to live with him while they attended college. Mac's friend, Justin, also lived with us, and so did Mac's new wife and their little girl. So, there were seven of us roommates in total.

Mac's house on Bank Street had plenty of room, though. It also had breathtaking views of Mt. Rainier. The scenery in Washington was gorgeous in general and unlike anything I was around growing up in Texas. Mac, being one of the most generous people in the world, didn't charge his family rent. He had a good job playing in the NFL, and he had invested wisely. He was happy to provide this experience for our two cousins and me.

He had a teammate, Justin, living in the guesthouse who did pay rent. Justin was not paying him anything at first because he didn't plan on staying very long. But he liked it at Mac's and we loved having him, so he moved into the guesthouse and started paying rent when Mac got married.

I knew the exact amount Justin paid because he told me. He and I talked all the time. He had been living with us for months, and in that time, we had adopted him into the family.

Justin could have easily bought his own place, but he chose to stay with us. He was a first-round draft pick who had sponsorships with five major brands and probably made about three times what my brother made in spite of Mac being a veteran player.

I, on the other hand, really appreciated the free rent. I was still in the building phase of my life. I had a job, and I was saving some and investing as much as I could, but there was no way I would be able to afford to live in the Mercer Island house if it didn't belong to my brother.

I bought groceries and I did my best to pull my weight. I cleaned some messes that weren't mine and I tried to be helpful with Mac's little stepdaughter, Victoria, who was three years old. I did not have to try very hard with her because she was an adorable little girl who was easy to be around.

Mac got married recently, and his wife, Morgan, moved into the main house with her little girl. Even then, both of them insisted that we all stay. Ozzy and Bri only had a year and a half left at college, and Mac and Morgan assumed they would continue to live with them until they were finished. Mac's house was gigantic, and he and Morgan truly did not mind having us around.

Needless to say, my brother was established in Seattle. He had been playing professional football for so long that there were only a handful of people on the team who had played there longer than him. Mac made a name for himself in Seattle, and the Seahawks loved him. Last season, they gave away Mac Klein bobble heads at one of the games.

I worked in sports also, but my job wasn't nearly as glamorous as Mac and Justin's. I went to college for Business Administration, and my first job was consulting for three of our family businesses back in Galveston. I was good at seeing the big picture of a business and seeing what needed to change to make things run more efficiently. My specialty was not necessarily making more money or selling products, but those things were a by-product of the changes I made.

Working at Bank Street Boxing with my uncle made me know that I would be interested in working as an athletic operations manager with a school or college. But unfortunately, there was nothing available in Seattle at the time I wanted to move. I looked for a job for months before I took a position as a production consultant at a large company that manufactured and installed home security systems.

I liked it okay and I made some nice friends there, but I left last month when I took another job running the sports office at Riverbend High School, the second largest senior high in Seattle.

I had longer hours now, and it was a thirty-minute drive from Mercer Island which doubled my commute every morning, but I loved it. I had only been there for two weeks, and I felt comfortable already. I was nervous and I had some big shoes to fill, but I trusted myself and didn't let the pressure get to me.

The gentleman who had been there before me had worked there for twenty years and was close to retirement age. This year, he and his wife went to their cabin in the woods for Christmas break, and he decided not to come back to work. The school was desperate to replace him on short notice, so I got the job even though I had a lot to learn.

Riverbend had programs for sports I did not even know existed when I was in high school. It was January, and we were supposed to hit the ground running with basketball, soccer, wrestling, baseball, softball, track and field, swim and dive, golf, volleyball, tennis, and lacrosse. There were also cheerleading, dance, and gymnastics programs. Each program had an established coaching staff, and the machine was already running, but my job was necessary.

I was a go-between for the media and the coaches. I handled conflicts with scheduling practice times and even did some mediating between coaches within different programs. I oversaw the athletic department from top to bottom, making sure that the grounds crew was on top of trash, lawn care, and general maintenance, and I made sure that the concessions were stocked and organized. It was a lot of management tasks, and it was the type of thing I really liked to do.

I had a lot to learn, but everyone was patient with me and seemed to be on my side. It was also a bonus for me to be in an academic setting. I was young at heart, and I liked cutting up with the students. I found it easy to be on good terms with students and faculty in spite of being new.

So, my work life was good, and my home life was good. But I was so exhausted from all the newness at work that I could hardly make time for a home life. It wouldn't always be like this, but for now, I was really busy. I was thinking about how busy I had been because I knew I would have to explain it to Morgan who was standing in the kitchen when I went downstairs.

"Well, hey," she said.

It was Friday morning at 10am—a time when I was not usually at home.

"Hey," I said to Morgan. "Hi, Victoria," I added when I came far enough into the room to see the little girl. The gorgeous, curly-haired girl glanced up at me with a smile and a wave before going back to playing with her toy. It was a fake dog, the plastic kind with a thin layer of fabric fur, the kind that used batteries to walk, sit, and bark.

"She's asking for a real dog, so we're trying this first," Morgan said when she saw me look down at the thing. It barked—a pre-recorded, high-pitched sound. I stared at Morgan who said, "Real puppies are at least that annoying." I made a face like I was about to take up for real puppies, and Morgan shook her head. "I love them as much as the next person. Seriously, I love puppies. But they take a lot of work. If I can't handle this little thing barking a few times, then I'm definitely not ready for a puppy."

"Yeah, I guess you're right," I said, staring at the barking plastic toy.

"I miss you," Morgan said. She lunged toward me and reached out for a hug, taking me by surprise.

"I miss you too," I said, smiling and hugging her back.

"Work has you busy, huh? Goodness."

I nodded. "Yeah. Between the commute and my hours at work, I feel like I'm never here anymore."

"I know. I was talking to Justin about it last night. He was asking about you—seeing if you were still going to the game. I couldn't believe he didn't know." She laughed. "Usually, Justin's the one telling me what's going on with you."

I laughed with her and shook my head. "I haven't seen any of y'all in what seems like all of January."

"Seriously," Morgan said. "I'm surprised I'm even seeing you right now."

"I know," I agreed. "But I'm staying for the basketball games tonight. I probably won't be home till after ten." I cocked my head at her. "Did you tell Justin I was going to the game?"

"Yes."

"He knew I was," I said. I shot her an injured glance, and she shrugged.

"Well, he wasn't sure with how busy you've been."

The game we were speaking about was in North Carolina. It was the game before the Super Bowl, an important football game. I always went to playoff games, but this was a big one. They would be playing in front of a sold-out crowd of 75,000 people. I got my plane tickets the day they found out where they were going. I felt a little hurt that Justin was acting like he didn't know if I'd be there. I didn't show it, though. I shrugged casually.

"That's one thing I'm learning about my job," I said. "They told me the guy who worked there before me didn't show up until one or two on game days." I sighed. "I'm not quite that brave. But I was thinking I'd get there around eleven today instead of eight. Those game days are too long."

"Did you sleep in this morning?" she asked, looking at me and noticing I was dressed for the day.

"Till eight-thirty," I said nodding. "Which feels really late. The principal knows how much I've been there lately. She said I should just take the day off and be at the game tonight, but I can't do it. I'm already stressing about getting over there, and it's not even... " I looked toward the clock.

"Ten-o-eight," Morgan said. The toy dog had gotten quiet, but he barked again when Victoria pushed a button. We both looked down, and Victoria looked up at us guiltily.

"Take it into the living room, and you can make all the noise you want," Morgan said.

Victoria picked up the dog and scampered off to the living room.

"What kind of game do you have to go to tonight? Basketball?"

"Yeah. Two of them, JV and varsity. They're having trouble with their ticketing system. They keep telling people to buy tickets online and they're having trouble."

"I like the school spirit," she said, pointing at my t-shirt, which said Riverbend Warriors across the front.

"Game day," I said. I had gone in there for breakfast so I went to the refrigerator and grabbed a single serving cup of yogurt.

I was fishing for a spoon when Morgan said, "I got some kind of entertainment news thing in my email, and the front page was talking about Heath Vick breaking up with Gwen Adams."

"They did," I said.

I let out an unintentional sigh. My year-long friendship with the A-list actor Heath Vick was complicated, and Morgan glanced at me like she didn't know how much I would say regarding his recent breakup.

Chapter 2

Justin chose that moment to appear. He came from the direction of the hallway rather than the guesthouse. But it only took a second for me to take in the clues and figure out that he had been swimming in Mac's indoor lap pool.

I smiled at him. "What's up, J-Money? Morgan didn't tell me you were back there."

"What's up with you, Lady Katie?"

I smiled at the sight of Justin who was like a brother to me since the day he moved in.

"Nothin'," I said. "I'm just eating yogurt and hanging out with Morgan and Vic for a second before I leave for work." I tilted my head at him when I thought of something. "Hey what's up with you asking if I was going to the game?"

Justin came into the kitchen with us. His hair was damp and he had a towel in his hand that looked like it was bundled around his wet bathing suit. He set the folded handful of clothes on the countertop before crossing to the fridge. Justin had on nice sweatpants and a tight white undershirt.

He was one of my best friends, so I didn't see him this way, but Justin was certainly what you would consider to be a ladies' man. He could basically get any woman he wanted. One of the students at Riverbend actually cried in front of me when she found out I knew him. She broke down and shed tears.

I was getting to know a few of the coaches and faculty at the school. I liked a lot of them, and I didn't tell a single soul that Justin was my roommate. That's how desirable he was—people would have behaved differently around me if they knew he was at my house every day when I left work. They knew that Mac was my brother, but no one knew that I lived with him or Justin.

"I didn't know if you were coming with how busy you've been," Justin said, responding to my question about the game. "I haven't seen you all week. I thought you were either working, or you went to New York to be with your boyfriend."

Everyone, especially Justin, gave me a hard time about being friends with Heath Vick.

"He's not my boyfriend, one, and two, it's not like I haven't seen you. Two nights ago, we sat here and watched The Office together until midnight."

"Yeah, but your car is barely ever in the driveway anymore," he said.

"I was just talking to Morgan about that," I said, moving to the other side of the kitchen to stand next to him.

Morgan could tell I was moving toward Justin, so she went into the living room to let us talk while she tended to Victoria.

"I've been going in at eight every morning, even when I stay for games, and it's just too much. In the future, I won't need to go to all of the games, but right now, I'm just taking stock of everything in the whole athletic program so I can know what needs to change. It's super time-consuming." I spoke in a regretful tone because I missed him.

Justin was quiet for a few seconds while he took a drink of juice. "You're just gonna blow past the whole Heath thing?"

Justin and I always spoke candidly with each other, so it didn't surprise me when he put me on the spot. I met Heath during the production of the movie that was based on my mother's book, Lox Island. Heath was the extremely famous actor who starred in that movie. His contract for Lox Island was for eleven million dollars. He was in a very public relationship with a famous actress.

Heath Vick had everything in the world, but for some reason, he liked me. He could have been impressed with me because of who my mother was. People seemed to be that way when they heard about her. He might have thought that as the daughter of a writer I was going to walk around correcting his grammar, and then he learned that I was a goofball, and he liked the contradiction.

We were friends, though. We never even saw each other off the movie set. We never texted or emailed. We only talked on the telephone. It was an odd sort of friendship. Heath had a lot of pressure and we were quick-witted with each other, making jokes and laughing a lot.

Heath was used to keeping up appearances. He was known for being a hot-looking guy, so he liked having a relationship with me that didn't at all revolve around looks. We were just friends. I gave him relief from the pressures of superstardom.

I did a bit of the same stuff for Justin and even my brother. I was a natural born encourager, like my brother, and I tried to create a positive environment around myself. My personality was perfect as a supporting player. I had learned that at Bank Street Boxing and I could see where my natural cheerleader mentality was going to be an asset with me working at the school.

That was why Heath liked me. I was real and candid with him and I didn't care at all about what he looked like. We were just friends.

Perhaps I should state it again.

We were just friends.

I never, ever wanted to be the other woman.

I, Katie Klein, was the main woman or no woman at all. I was not trying to replace Gwen and honestly, this recent break up was a surprise to me. Heath told me he was going to do it, but not until right before.

Things had been slightly different with him lately. We were talking less because of how busy I was with work these last few weeks, and then, Heath just out of the blue said he was leaving Gwen.

He moved out of their apartment the following day, and during the next week, it was all over the tabloids. This whole incident was recent, so I was half-expecting to be questioned about it from my roommates.

I stood beside Justin and rubbed my face. I let out a little groan, thinking about how complicated everything was with Heath. I wasn't ready to think about breakups or contemplate how he would move on. He had mentioned wanting to fly me out to New York, but he never came right out and said he wanted to change the relationship he had with me.

"I'm not trying to blow past it," I said to Justin. "There's just nothing to tell."

"I hope you know that if he got with you by cheating on her, then he'll get with someone else while he's cheating on you."

"What?" I asked, cocking my head to the side and giving him an offended glare. "I don't know what's wrong with you, but that was just mean."

"I'm not being mean, I'm just telling the truth. If he cheated on his last girlfriend, he'll probably cheat on his next one."

"Well, no one ever said I was his girlfriend," I said defensively.

It made me sick to think about being the other woman. It gave me a stomachache to think that Justin saw it that way.

"We don't even flirt on the phone," I said. "We are straight-up friends… like me and you." I shuffled to stand in front of him in a playful boxing stance and performed a light hook, barely touching his arm with my fist. I had attended years of boxing classes. The sport ran through my veins, and it felt natural for me to shift around on my toes, shadowboxing. Justin reached out and batted me away, giving me a half smile and shaking his head. He looked like a male model in that undershirt. He had these perfect blue eyes and he cut them at me.

"I'm just saying, Katie. I don't care who you go out with, but I'd be careful with that dude."

"I am being careful. We're just friends, like I said. I mean, who wouldn't want to be friends with Heath Vick?"

"I wouldn't," Justin said.

"Well, like, ninety-percent of other people would," I said.

"Why? Just because he's famous?"

"Yeah, I guess. But he's super famous, Justin. Even more than you, and that's saying something. People freak out about both of you. Some girl cried right in front of me when I told her I was friends with you."

"What girl?"

"A girl at my school. A student. A teenager."

"Did you tell her you were friends with Heath Vick?" he asked.

"No, goodness, no," I said. "Nobody knows that."

"Why not?"

"Because they'd never leave me alone about it. And it's not like we're that close. We don't ever even see each other."

"How often do you talk to him?"

I hesitated. I opened my mouth to say the truth, but then I thought twice about it and changed my mind.

"Just tell me," Justin said. "It's not like I care."

I shrugged. "I don't really keep track, but before he and Gwen broke up, maybe once or twice a week, maybe three times, something like that. But since then it's been a little more often."

"Like what?"

"I don't know. He's been texting me a little bit, too."

"Do you like him?" Justin asked the question so casually that I knew he didn't care.

"Yeah, I mean, who wouldn't, right? But it's not like he broke up with Gwen for me or anything."

"What makes you say that?" he asked.

"Because we live on opposite sides of the country. We never even talk about that kind of stuff. We're just friends." Justin shot me a sarcastic look, to which I said, "What?"

"You're turning red just talking about him."

"Stop it," I said.

I wasn't turning red. Justin was just giving me a hard time.

"I miss you," I said.

Justin nodded as he finished a glass of juice that he had poured from the fridge. "I know, KK, I miss you, too," he said. "Why do you have to work so much?"

"Coming from the guy who is working out before he goes to work." I pointed toward the pool, knowing that Justin had been in there swimming to work out a hamstring strain.

"I'm feeling a little better," he said. "I'm just stretching it out after yesterday's practice. I'm heading to the airport in a couple of minutes."

"I knew you were leaving soon," I said. "I was going to run out to your house to say goodbye if I hadn't seen you in here."

"When are you getting to Charlotte?" he asked.

"Tomorrow at three," I said.

"We can hang out tomorrow night," he said. "Get some dinner. I'm sure Mac and Morgan will want to do something."

"Yeah, that sounds good. I assumed we would," I said. "And we have to get your gummy bears."

(Justin ate a certain brand of gummy bears before big games.)

"They'll have them at the field," he said. "Perry made sure they would have them there."

"Okay, because I can stop at this little flower shop before I leave town if you want. I saw that brand in there the other day."

"No, it's all good, they'll have them at the field. They're rolling out the red carpet for us." He paused and cocked his head at me. "Why are you all dressed up like a cheerleader?" he asked. His eyes roamed down to my shirt, which had shrunk a little in the dryer and felt tighter than shirts I usually wore.

I squirmed a little. I was already self-conscious about it so the cheerleader comment made me tug at the fabric.

"Don't stretch it out. What are you doing? It looks good. I like it. Leave it alone." Justin looked me over. "I've just never seen you wear one like that with the stripes on the sleeves."

"Yeah, I'm going to a basketball game tonight, and technically this is a football shirt, but I didn't think anyone would care." I paused before adding, "Just so you know, I care about family values."

Justin made a confused face. "Where did that come from?"

"You were asking me about Heath, and I just didn't want you to think I broke them up. I met Gwen at the screening, and she was a really nice person."

"Did she know you guys talked on the phone before they broke up?"

"I don't know. I don't know what he talked to Gwen about. But we weren't doing or saying anything that needed to be hidden."

"Okay, fine, it doesn't matter. But the fact remains that he broke up with his wife and now he's calling you every day."

"She wasn't his wife," I said.

"Whatever. They were together a long time."

"I see what you're saying, but it's not like that."

"What do you mean, it's not like that? There's no other way to interpret it. They broke up, and now you talk to him every day."

"I talk to *you* every day," I said.

"You used to," he said.

"Still, not that it matters, but Heath and I are just friends. We talk about music and books and TV. We don't flirt with each other. In fact, last night he brought up this other girl, somebody who's re-doing the closets in his new apartme... I don't know why I'm telling you any of this. We're just friends."

Chapter 3

I arrived in North Carolina the following afternoon.

I was on a flight with Morgan, Victoria, and some other wives and family that had come in from Seattle. We were delayed, so I barely had enough time to change and make it to dinner.

Morgan and Mac decided not to go to dinner with us. They made plans to eat at the hotel and let Victoria swim in the pool. I got dinner with Justin and about five others—two other guys from the team, and a few people that were traveling with them. Mac had been playing in Seattle for eight seasons, so I had already met all of the people that went to dinner with us. All season, I had been Justin's sidekick, and no one was surprised to see us together.

We ate at an expensive steak house, and Justin picked up the tab. I knew he was going to do it, so I ordered brussels sprouts and a side of mac and cheese. I looked at the ticket when it was in his lap, and the total for all of us was over a thousand dollars.

"Thank you," I said a while later when we were on our way back to the hotel and it was just the two of us. It was after eight o'clock, and the guys had to be at the field early the following morning for a twelve o'clock game.

I had heard some news from Heath while we were eating dinner earlier, but I didn't mention it to Justin. Heath was going to come to the game the following day. He tried to call me but I didn't pick up, so he told me in a text. We had been at dinner, talking to people, so I didn't even have time to think about it until now. Justin and I rode up the elevator toward our rooms and I debated telling him.

"Which room are you in?" I asked instead. I didn't have anything to hide, but I also didn't feel like bringing up Heath. I opted not to say anything about it. Justin would be busy tomorrow, anyway.

"Fifteen-twenty-two."

"Twenty-two like you," I said, talking about his jersey number.

"Yeah."

"All right. I'm bunking with my parents, so you could come in there with us if you want."

"Are your parents up?" he asked.

"Yeah," I said. "But it's a suite, so they've got their own bedroom and everything."

"I'll come in for a while, then," Justin agreed.

And he did. We were such good friends that this type of thing was a normal occurrence. Justin had latched onto our family when he moved in with Mac. He came to Mac's wedding in Texas, and he was always with us when we were in Seattle.

Justin's family was small and most of them lived in Oakland. None of them made it out for this game. His parents would have normally tried to be there, but his dad had broken his heel falling off of a ladder and was still recovering. Justin said if they won tomorrow and made it to the Super Bowl, they would try to make it. He had been on his own all through college and for two years since, so he didn't seem to mind that they weren't there.

He loved hanging out with our family, though, because he could be himself. He ran to his room and changed into sweatpants before coming back to my parents' room. We watched Diners, Drive-ins, and Dives and other food television shows for three hours. We talked some and stayed silent some, and I was as comfortable in front of him as I was with my own family. My brother had several close football-friends over the years, but I was tighter with Justin than I had been with any of them.

He told me everything, and vice versa, which is why it was weird to hold back the fact that Heath would be at the game tomorrow. We spent hours together, and I decided not to tell him. I wasn't afraid that he'd be upset about it, but I wanted him to be in a good headspace for the game tomorrow, and it just never seemed like a good time to bring up Heath.

I told him goodnight at eleven o'clock and he walked down the hall to his own room.

I didn't see Justin or my brother the following morning. They had to report to the field bright and early, and I knew we wouldn't connect before the game.

We left early, too. We went to the field in plenty of time to find our box. Our family included several famous people, so I knew the live broadcast would pan to us sometime during the game. It was for this reason that I spent extra time doing my hair and makeup. I didn't wear a lot, but I did a careful job of applying it and arranging my hair. My mom was right there in the room with me, so she braided two parts of it back, and the rest, I wore down. We would have access to a room in our suite that was closed to the cameras and the elements, but I liked to sit outside and watch the game. It was January, so I bundled up.

I told Heath what suite we were in at the arena, and he showed up there. You needed a pass just to ride the elevator that took you to the level with the suites. Heath didn't ask me for a ticket, and yet somehow, he showed up at the door of our suite ten minutes before kickoff.

He had his friend with him. I had met Ben one other time. He wasn't technically a bodyguard, he was more like a friend who hung around all the time and was big, tough, and knew martial arts. Ben was with Heath constantly, and sure enough, they both showed up at the door just before the game started.

My family was all really nice to him, but I couldn't converse with him like he expected me to. Justin was the star running back which meant he was in most of the offensive plays. He did fine on the field, and he ran at full power, but when he came off,

I could see him favoring one side. He wasn't limping, but I knew he was pushing past something out there.

That, combined with the fact that it was an intense game, made me act preoccupied around Heath. Thankfully, some others in our suite picked up my slack and kept Heath entertained. He was, however, sitting next to me when they showed our box seats on the jumbotron and on the national broadcast. They gave us a heads up that they were going to do it. Heath smiled and waved at the camera, and we heard live yells from adoring fans in the stadium. I smiled and looked normal, but I was more interested in watching the game.

It was a close game, and we fought hard, but we lost. There were twenty or thirty of us in the suite, and we all had tentative plans to eat out afterward. We were assuming the Hawks would win, and that we would be celebrating, but tonight it hadn't worked out that way.

We had reservations, though, so we decided to go eat. Justin came with us and so did one other player, a guy from Cuba who didn't have any family at the game. Heath and Ben sat next to me, but there was nothing going on between us—no flirting—just hanging out with my family.

Justin rode to the restaurant with Mac and Carlos, and they met us there. We had been to enough post-loss meals that we knew the guys would be in quiet moods.

There were over twenty of us in a private room at the restaurant. There was talking, but it was laid-back and mostly in groups of two or three people who were sitting next to one another.

Mac, Justin, and Carlos were the last ones to arrive, and their chairs were positioned on the other side of the U-shaped table where they were looking at my back. I was next to Heath, and we never looked behind us. My parents and my little brother, Andrew, were sitting all around us, along with Uncle Evan and his family. We focused on them rather than turning around.

I wanted to talk to Justin, though.

I wanted to check on his leg.

I kept wanting to turn around, but I just couldn't make myself.

We were almost done with our meal when two people who were sitting behind us, my cousin Bri and her mom, Aunt Tara, got up to use the restroom. I knew because Bri hit my purse as she walked by. It was hanging on the back of my chair and she hit it so hard that she stopped in her tracks.

"Oh, I'm so sorry," Bri said looking down at me. "I wasn't even looking where I was going."

"It's okay," I said, smiling at her over my shoulder.

She was a fan of Heath, even before he and I started talking, so she smiled at him. I glanced at the table behind us while I was turned around. Bri and Aunt Tara's absence left a gap and I now had a clear view of my brother and Justin. Justin glanced my way, and I gave him a quick half smile, meeting his gaze. My cousin, Ozzy, was on one side of him and Mac was on the other. Carlos had moved halfway through the meal to sit on the end, next to my cousin, Nick, who spoke Spanish.

"Heath, did you meet Justin and Mac?" Ozzy asked just after I made eye contact with Justin.

Heath had turned around and was looking at the guys as well. I was aware of it, but I couldn't see him because I was looking over my right shoulder and he was on my left. Ozzy liked Heath and had spent a lot of time with him during the game, so it didn't surprise me that he spoke directly to Heath from across the table.

"I haven't met Justin or Carlos," Heath said, projecting his voice and shifting in his chair to better face the people behind us. I could hear and feel him adjusting behind me.

"Justin's the one I was telling you about with the diet plan," Ozzy said. "You'll have to come to Seattle and stay at the house sometime. He's got a chef who comes in three times a week."

Justin turned to look at Ozzy with a straight face. "He doesn't care about coming to Seattle," Justin said, not smiling. "And Mac doesn't have room for all that." Justin stared at Ozzy who was sitting next to him. He wasn't speaking loudly, but I had a clear view of him, and I could hear him just enough to make out what he was saying. He was being a little rude, and I didn't want Heath to hear him. I turned around, shifting in my chair to look over the other shoulder so I could see Heath.

"Whoa, wow, he's a friendly fella," Heath said in a sarcastic tone. He spoke at a low volume. But I still glanced back at Justin to make sure he hadn't heard.

Ozzy, who wasn't used to Justin behaving this way, gave him a curious smile and head tilt like he thought Justin was joking.

Justin just shrugged and looked at me and Heath with an expressionless stare before starting to eat his food again.

I turned away from him. "It was a hard loss," I explained to Heath in a quiet tone once we turned our backs to Ozzy and Justin. "They're always quiet after a tough loss. It's the end of the season, and, you know, they leave it all out on the field, and it's just a quiet night for them all."

"Yeah, I get it," Heath said. "I was just messing around about him being in a bad mood. I wasn't expecting your cousin to try to introduce us."

"How's the fish?" my mom asked Heath.

They knew each other pretty well from him starring in the movie, so she had talked to him the whole time at dinner. I went along with their conversation about fish, and I acted like nothing was bothering me, but it was.

I wished I could check on Justin. I hated that one friend was making it awkward for me to be good to another friend.

Chapter 4

Three months later
April

"Hey, Miss Klein, are you coming to our baseball game tonight?"

I heard a male voice from behind me and heard footsteps. I turned to find Henry Young, a senior athlete, coming toward me in the otherwise empty hallway.

"I can't," I said in a tone that made it clear I couldn't budge. "I've got a crazy week ahead of me starting as soon as I leave here today."

"What do you have going on?" Henry asked.

He came up beside me. I was carrying five boxes of candy, and he took three of them off of the top of my stack like the gentleman he was.

"You don't have to," I said. "I'm just going to the golf cart, and it's right here by the door."

"It's fine," he said. "Are you headed to the field with this? Because I could use a ride over there, anyway."

"Yeah, come on," I said, walking with him. "I wish I could come to the game, but I can't make it to this one."

"What are you doing working at a high school and hauling boxes of Skittles around, Miss Klein?" Henry asked out-of-nowhere.

I turned to him with a curious expression. "What do you mean? Somebody's got to haul them."

"Why you, though? Didn't your mom write Harry Potter? I thought someone like you didn't have to work a normal job."

I let out a little laugh at how hard I had been working at this job lately. "It's Lox Island," I said.

"Oh, well, same difference," he said.

"Well, even still… my parents aren't… they have three kids and, I don't know, they want us to all have our own life and our own experiences. They have money and I know I can go to them if I get in a bind, but I never thought that having them pay for everything was an option." We stacked boxes of candy onto the back of the golf cart. "And I don't mind hauling candy," I said. "This needs to get over there, and I need to see how the grounds crew did painting the dugouts."

"Oh, they look great," Henry said. "I was just over there."

"Good," I said.

I started the golf cart and took off toward the field with Henry sitting next to me. "What are you doing this weekend?" he asked, as we drove.

I took my eyes off the road long enough to glance at him with a curious expression. "Why?"

"You said back there that you have a crazy week starting when you leave here. I was wondering what you're doing."

"Oh that, I'm..." I paused because the truth was that my busy week started with me going to a film festival with Heath. "My Brother and his wife are going to Hawaii and I volunteered to watch their little girl. I took off three days next week since I'll have her."

This was the truth, I just left out the part about flying to Canada beforehand to meet Heath for a day. It was already enough for these kids that my mom was Lucy Klein, and then Mac and Justin—they would freak out if they knew I had been friends with Heath Vick this whole time. I knew not to talk about Heath.

Henry was a three-sport athlete and would probably be more impressed that I was friends with Justin than he would be with Heath. I didn't talk about either of them, though. It was just a self-given and self-enforced policy.

"Babysitting?" Henry asked as we drove past the parking lot, headed for the baseball field.

"Yeah. My brother and his wife are going to Hawaii, and I told them I'd keep their little girl. I have roommates, and my cousins are there to help me out, but I'm mostly in charge."

"Are you coming to our game against South Kitsap?"

"It's next Friday, right?"

"Yeah," he said. "It's senior night, too."

"I'll be there," I promised. "My brother should be back by then, and if not, Victoria can just come to the game with me."

"Good," he said. "Also, if we win, we're going to put a pie in Coach Brown's face."

"Yeah, you don't want to do that if you lose," I said.

"He'd murder us at practice if we did that," Henry said, shaking his head.

I had a ton of questions for him about that whole pie idea, including how, when, and where they were going to get the actual pie, but I didn't ask. I figured he had a plan. I wasn't going to stress about it. I needed to leave, anyway, to get to the airport.

"All right Henry. Have fun tonight," I said, stopping in front of the gate that led to the field.

"I was going to help you put up the candy," he said, pointing straight ahead to the concession stand.

"Thanks, but I've got it," I said.

Henry got out and patted the top of the golf cart before he jogged in front of it.

"Thanks, for the ride, Katherine," he said.

Henry and a few of the other seniors teased me ever since they learned my first name. They saw it written somewhere, and they got the biggest kick out of it. "You're very welcome, Henry," I said, unaffected. I smiled and shook my head at him as I took off. "Y'all win today!" I yelled, over my shoulder as I drove.

"We will!" he yelled back as he disappeared into the gate.

I was in Canada by 8pm that evening.

I went through a lot of rushing and driving and getting dressed, but considering that those things were normal travel activities, it was a smooth trip.

The flight from Seattle to Vancouver was only an hour, and there was a car waiting for me at the airport.

I went to dinner in Heath's hotel room. It was a gigantic suite, and he had an entourage there, so it felt more like a restaurant than a hotel room. I had heard Heath talk about a few of the people that were there, but Ben was the only one I had met before this. They were all nice, though, and we stayed in there for a while.

All of us were staying on the floor right below Heath, and we left at the same time. We had already settled on plans for tomorrow. In the morning, we were seeing some cherry blossoms and then, at noon, we would watch a movie that Heath's best friend directed.

Niall was his name, and he was walking next to me as we went to the elevator after leaving Heath's.

One group had already gone down, and another group of four got on the elevator as Niall and I lagged behind, talking in the hallway.

"Go ahead," he said to them.

Niall had asked me a question about my great uncle who was a famous boxer back in the seventies.

"He still has a gym in Galveston," I said.

"And, did I hear you say that's where you grew up?"

"Yeah," I said.

The elevator closed completely, and we approached the wall and pushed the button to call for another one.

"I guess we could just go down the stairs," I said, laughing a little. "It wouldn't kill us to walk down one flight."

"That's all right," he said. "I don't climb any stairs if I don't have to."

I didn't remind him that we were going down and not up, and therefore wouldn't be climbing any stairs. He already knew that.

"So, do you do any boxing?"

"I do, actually. I did. I went to class twice a week when I was living in Galveston. It's been almost a year since I moved in with Mac, and I haven't put on my gloves once. He has a heavy bag in his home gym, but I never go do any rounds on it." I paused and nodded. "I need to, now that we mention it. I'll probably work out some when I get back home tomorrow—just to knock the dust off that bag."

I was talking to be friendly, so I was happy when the elevator dinged and the door opened. We stepped inside, and I pushed the button to take us down to the floor below.

Niall took a small piece of paper out of his pocket and held it out for me to take. I reached out for it instinctually, looking at him for an explanation. I could feel that it was an envelope for a credit card shaped object.

"This is to Heath's room," he said, speaking so quietly and stiffly that I assumed he thought there were cameras in the elevator.

"Am I supposed to whisper?" I asked with a stiff wide-eyed expression.

"Yes," he said a little impatiently as if my current volume wasn't low enough.

"What's this for?" I asked, barely moving my mouth, but looking straight at him."

"Heath's room," he whispered. "He said for you to shower and get yourself ready for him, and come to his room at midnight."

My heart started pounding instantly. I knew it wasn't that serious, but I felt trapped suddenly, like I had gotten myself into something that I would regret—that I already regretted. I pushed the envelope back toward Niall, trying to seem cool.

"That's okay," I said. "I was just planning on seeing him tomorrow for breakfast with you guys."

His expression remained serious. I couldn't tell exactly what he was feeling, but he looked a little stunned. He shook his head.

"Well, he's expecting you, so… "

"So?"

"So, I did my part. You can work it out with him," he said, pushing the envelope back toward me and giving me a fake smile.

I glanced up, assuming we were on camera. I didn't see anything up there, but I only looked for a second. I returned his smile with a stiff, freaked-out looking one of my own. The door opened, but I didn't want to leave with Niall thinking I was going to go to Heath's room.

"I'm just going to text him and..."

"Sure," he said, nodding and cutting me off.

"Midnight... and use the stairs." Niall spoke in a low tone, even after we had stepped out of the elevator and into the hall.

His room was down a different hallway because he branched off near the elevator and went down the hallway to the right.

I couldn't let him walk away having the last word. "I'll see you guys in the morning," I said.

I was left holding the room key even though I wasn't going to use it. I was shaking as I walked. I dug in my purse and found my own room key. Two other people who had been in Heath's room with us were still talking in the hall, but I ignored them and went straight into my room.

Heath and I had behaved like we were just friends this entire time, so this gesture with the room key felt totally unexpected, and unwelcome. It rubbed me the wrong way that he told me to take a shower, and I leaned down and sniffed my own armpit to see if I stunk, which I didn't.

I set down my purse with a sigh, feeling dirty. I couldn't believe he would think it would be that easy. He was expecting me to go up there and... *for things to happen with us, right? Was that what I was supposed to assume from what Niall said?* I took out my phone and stared at it, knowing I would send a text to Heath and contemplating what I would say in it.

Chapter 5

Justin Teague

Justin had been living with Mac for almost a year, and during that time he had gotten close to Mac and all three of his family members who lived at the house on Mercer Island. The house had views of Mt. Rainier, and the surroundings and company were beautiful and comfortable. He was currently floating near the edge of the gorgeous, zero entry salt water swimming pool in Mac's backyard. It was cool out, but the pool was heated.

Justin's family was in California, so Mac had basically adopted him. Mac had a sister named Katie, and she had become one of his best friends.

Mac met his wife, Morgan, soon after Justin moved in, and their relationship was fast and time-consuming. Justin still saw Mac a lot at work, but Katie and Justin spent a ton of time together at home. That had changed a little since she got the job at the high school and started working more.

Justin was currently with another woman, someone Katie had introduced him to. But it was Katie he was thinking about.

"Katie," he said.

"Why are you thinking about Katie?" she asked. It was Gretchen, one of Katie's friends from her previous job. Gretchen was an accomplished pianist, she was gorgeous, and she had a good job as a marketing manager at a large company. On top of it all, she was a nice person. She could cook and she could carry on a pleasant conversation. She was single, and she was a perfect replacement for Katie.

"Why were you thinking about Katie?" Gretchen asked.

"Because Mac's leaving in the morning and we'll have Victoria."

"Oh, yeah, Katie told me she was babysitting this weekend. I didn't realize you were helping her."

"Yeah. We all promised Mac."

"I'm surprised Morgan didn't want to have her mom come in to watch her."

"She did want to. She mentioned that, but we told her we wanted to do it. KK's been so busy with work that it'll do her good to take a few days off and chill with Victoria."

"What about the dad's mom?" Gretchen asked.

Justin nodded. "Mac's mom offered, too. She said she'd fly in from Galveston to help, but like I said, Katie wanted to do it."

"I meant the other dad."

Justin knew she meant Tyson Richardson, Victoria's real dad who had passed away. Justin knew a lot about him. Tyson was a running back just like Justin, only he was a few years older. Justin had studied his footage in college and had been compared to him by commentators since he entered the league.

"Yeah. Tyson didn't have anybody," Justin said, knowing the whole story. "His dad was never around, and his mom died when he was in high school."

He smiled and shrugged at Gretchen. "But both of the other moms volunteered to help out, and Katie didn't want either of them to come. She insisted. But I think it'll be good for her. She's been working a ton."

"How many days do you guys have to keep her?" Gretchen asked.

"Six, but Katie's off work for five of them, and Bri took off on day six, which is a half-day, anyway, so I don't think I'll have to ever even be alone with her. I'm just here to help out. It's for that trip Mac and Morgan won on the Lexi show."

Gretchen giggled as she swam up next to him, starting up at him with adoring eyes.

"He didn't *win* anything," she said, correcting him. "She just gave it to them for going on her show. She does that with all her guests. One time, she gave away a new house."

Justin shrugged like it didn't matter.

"I can't believe Katie's in Canada with Heath Vick right now," Gretchen said.

"Why can't you believe it?" Justin asked, sounding completely aloof even though everything about Heath Vick annoyed him.

"Because. Just imagine. What if they get married?"

Justin scoffed.

"What?" Gretchen asked.

"They would never get married," he said.

"Why not?"

"Because she would not marry somebody like that."

Gretchen laughed. "Oh, you think he would marry her but she wouldn't marry him?" She grinned as if she saw a ton of humor in that thought, and Justin just shook his head. "I can see what you're saying about Katie, though," Gretchen said. "She's picky. But she has some appeal—some different, quirky appeal."

"I think she's got regular appeal," Justin said.

"You know what I mean," Gretchen said, swimming close to him again. "She's quirky, you can't deny it. Just the way she dresses, and the way she… says whatever is on her mind, even if it's not the… most intelligent thing to say."

Gretchen sounded lighthearted and she was smiling, but she was taking digs at Katie, and it irked Justin. He didn't smile back.

"I don't really know what you mean," he said, thinking that Katie would never say those same things about Gretchen.

"I mean all I'm saying is that from an outsider's perspective, Katie better not miss her chance to be with somebody like Heath."

"Maybe. But we're not outsiders, so we can see that she's the one who's actually too good for him." Justin spoke easily in a no-nonsense tone.

"Yeah, I guess," Gretchen said, not sounding convinced. "But I still recommend that she go ahead and lock that down this weekend."

"What's that mean?" he asked.

She smiled and shrugged as she hovered in the shallows next to him. She bit her lip shyly. "You know, I'm sure they... you're the one who said they talk all the time. And you don't just go on a trip with somebody, and not think that it's going to lead to—"

"Yes, you do," Justin said, cutting her off before she could say more. "She's just friends with that dude. I don't even know what you're saying right now. Katie would never go over there and..." Justin trailed off, partly because he was uncertain of what to say. "She's coming home tomorrow," he said. He spoke in a normal tone even though his heart was racing. He had made these plans with Gretchen when he heard that Katie would be out of town, and he now regretted it. The things Gretchen was saying about Katie made him feel differently about her, and he didn't feel like hanging out with her anymore.

"There's no way she's..." he spoke out loud before he thought of what he was going to say.

"No way she's what?" Gretchen asked when Justin trailed off.

"She wouldn't do that," he said. But Gretchen had planted a seed of doubt, and Justin started to worry. "And she'd be sad if she knew you assumed that," he added, trying to keep Gretchen from saying anything else about it.

"Jesus, Justin, I guess I assumed you weren't going to tell her." Gretchen smiled at him as she said it. She thought she was being so cute, and Justin didn't like it at all. She used that name casually, like a lighthearted exclamation, so maybe it shouldn't have stuck out to him, but it did. Justin wasn't what you would classify as being prudish or closed minded. He had been in locker rooms his whole life and had heard the Lord's name used in that type of context and much worse. He wasn't trying to judge Gretchen. But he couldn't help that it made her less attractive to him. He stared at her, thinking *Katie would never say that.*

This wasn't the first time he compared them. Katie had been the one to introduce Justin to Gretchen, so that was probably why he always compared the two. Gretchen was beautiful, and she was a great girl. But it was those subtle differences, like Katie's innocence, that made Justin know he ultimately wouldn't settle down with Gretchen. He didn't mean to judge her, and perhaps he could have talked it out with her, but a switch had been flipped that evening, and Justin wondered what he was even doing there with her in the pool.

He felt Gretchen's hand on his side and he shifted away from the edge of the pool. He tried to make it look like he was already doing that when she touched him, but it was obvious.

"What's the matter with you?" she asked.

"Nothing, I was already coming over here." Justin started to say something else to smooth things over with Gretchen, but then he wondered why he wanted to make the effort if this wasn't going anywhere. He used his hand to wipe his face and sighed, knowing there was no easy way to do this.

"I think I'm going to go up to the gym instead of hanging out tonight," he said. "My mind's just... in the game right now."

It was a lie, but he didn't know what else to say.

"I need to go drill," he added. He wasn't lying about that part. His heart was about to beat out of his chest, and he would end up working out since that was what he did every time he needed to blow off steam.

His mind was buzzing.

Katie was his friend.

A friend was all she was.

He tried to tell himself that, but he despised Heath Vick and everyone else who would keep him from Katie. *Why did he all of a sudden feel like he had to have her? Was it just because Gretchen was there and he was comparing the two of them?*

"What about ordering food?" Gretchen asked.

But Justin climbed out of the pool.

"I thought we said we were getting sushi in a minute," she said, smiling up at him and obviously not understanding how serious he was about her leaving.

"No, no, I'm sorry, Gretchen, but I'll be heading out in just a few minutes. I just remembered something I wanted to do. I need to get some stuff done."

"Are you *mad* at me?" she asked, looking hurt and confused.

"No," Justin said. "I'm sorry. No. I've just… changed my mind about what I'm doing tonight, so I'm ready to get going now."

Gretchen started climbing out of the pool.

Justin held out a towel for her, but she took her time getting to him. She came out of the water, step-by-step, taking her time, letting the water drip off of her body. She was smiling and walking slowly, posing, waiting for Justin to look at her.

He held the towel between them just right where he couldn't see her from the neck to the knees. He liked Gretchen, and he was sorry to admit it, but this whole flirty bit came off as really desperate. There were only four or five steps in the shallow end of the pool, and it took her forever to fully get out.

Justin wondered if it was wrong to pray for patience in a situation he had gotten himself into. He reminded himself that he was the one who had texted Gretchen and asked her over. It was by his invitation that she was there. She stared at him as she took the towel. She had been trying to seduce him the whole way out of the pool, and it seemed to finally sink in that he wasn't going for it.

Her hopeful expression fell, and she snatched the towel from him disappointedly. "Is this really a thing where you suddenly have to go to the gym, or are you just telling me that and you're really never going to call me back?" she asked.

Justin felt taken aback by the honest question, and he stuttered. "I-I'm, you're friends with Katie, so I'm sure I'll see you, when you're with her. I'm sorry, Gretchen." She looked injured, and it made Justin feel bad enough to say, "I might call you back. I don't know. I don't know what I'm thinking right now, I'm sorry."

Chapter 6

Katie
That same evening

I was probably insane for being turned off by
Heath's forward proposition.

Maybe most women would love for a guy to say
she should go shower for him. Maybe I was weird
for not liking it. But I didn't care for being told to go
take a shower. That wasn't my style of... whatever it
was Heath was trying to make happen.

It was almost 11pm and I still hadn't texted him
to let him know I wasn't coming to his room at
midnight. I hadn't done it because I wasn't sure of
what I was going to say. At first, I composed a text
trying to let him down easy. I lied and said that I had
a stomachache and told him I hoped to feel better
and see him in the morning.

Then I deleted that one and composed another
one that was completely honest and candid, saying
that I wasn't a type of girl who easily spent the night
in guys' rooms. That second one was a nice-
knowing-ya type of text, which I also deleted.

I composed two others and deleted those as well.

I didn't know what I wanted to say to Heath.

It was fun being friends with someone as famous
as he was. His face was on tabloids and movie

posters, and it felt good to have him notice me, like me, invite me places. Part of me wanted to preserve our relationship, and the other part wanted to end it. I was so fifty-fifty with it that I put off sending a text.

I thought about just not texting at all and showing up at his door when he expected me to. I wasn't going to let things happen between us, but I wondered if it would be better for me to explain things in person. I thought that if I explained it in a text, he might get mad at me and I might never see him again.

I wondered if I even wanted to see him again.

I took a shower and took off my makeup, knowing that even if I walked up there and talked to him face-to-face, I wasn't looking to impress him or cause him to be attracted to me. I wasn't even sure if I wanted to go to the festival with him, or to breakfast in the morning.

Heath was constantly surrounded with people, so he would hardly notice my absence.

I agonized over it for a while before I remembered to pray and ask God's advice.

"I don't know what to do," I said out loud.

I sat in the bed, staring blankly at the television, which was on mute.

"I need advice. I need You to tell me what to do. I don't know how to tell him I'm not going up there. Or should I go up there? What if Heath's the one? Am I messing up if I mess things up with him?"

Even as I asked that last question, I knew in my heart that Heath wasn't the one, but I kept talking to God.

"I wish there was a way that You could audibly tell me what to do."

I took a deep breath, wishing I had the answer and staring at the television. I distractedly thought of orange juice since there was a commercial for it on the screen.

I wanted a glass of orange juice.

My mouth was dry.

I had just remembered that I was in the middle of a prayer, and I was about to get back to saying it when I heard my phone ring.

My nerves experienced a jolt when I heard it.

I thought it might be Heath, and I tried to make a split-second decision about what excuse I would say to him.

Relief washed over me like cool water when I saw Justin's name on my screen. I might as well have been riding an innertube on a lazy river with how relaxed I was when I saw his name.

I smiled and pressed the button to answer the call with no hesitation whatsoever. "Wuzzzuuuup!" I said in the most laid-back tone possible. My voice was deep with full-on relaxation. I was ecstatic that it was Justin and not Heath, and it came across in my voice.

"What's up with you?" Justin asked. "Where are you?"

"Canada. Where are you?"

"I'm at the house," he said. "Where I should be."

"I know, I saw you on Gretchen's Instagram earlier."

"What'd you see?" he asked.

"Just y'all at the pool. She was in the pool and you were in the background, over by that mosaic table."

"That was when I was talking to Ozzy."

"Oh. He wasn't in the picture. She might've cropped it."

"I didn't even know she took that picture. She left right after that. What are you doing?"

"I'm just hanging out in my hotel room, watching TV and stuff."

"I thought you'd be with Heath," he said.

I started to say one thing, and then I changed my mind and let out a breath.

"What?" he said.

"Nothing. It's fun. We hung out with about ten other people the whole time. Tomorrow, we're supposed to wake up and see a bunch of these Japanese Cherry Blossom trees and then Niall has a movie premiering at noon."

"Sounds artsy."

"I don't think it's that big of a deal," I said. "It's a small film festival. It's not the famous one you think of when you think of Vancouver. That happens in the fall. This is Niall's first film. Some of the actors were hanging out with us tonight, and they were all new to it and excited about the premier and everything. How did your workout go?" I asked, changing the subject. "How's your leg?"

"It's fine. I'm feeling okay."

"What'd Greg say about those cleats?" I asked.

"He said he thinks they're unrelated. He thinks I'm still working out that injury. I'm still going to try a new pair—see if I can get some better support."

"I think it's a good idea," I said. "I heard one of the trainers talking to Henry the other day about something similar—that a foot problem could be causing a strain somewhere else."

"Yeah," he said. "I guess athletes are kind of all chasing injuries."

"The best ones usually are," I said.

"What time are you getting home tomorrow?" he asked.

"I think around six. Bri's watching Victoria because Mac and Morgan fly out at three and my flight doesn't get in until later. But I'm parked in a good spot at the airport, so I'll be right home. Are you going to be there?"

"Yeah, I talked to Mac already. I'll be around all week. It's all good. She'll do fine. You know how easygoing she is. I could probably keep her by myself."

"Yeah, and she's going to never leave her toys with that tree house you bought."

Justin had asked me to pick out a toy set. He gave me his credit card, and I ordered a wooden tree house with a whole set of different woodland creatures. It was a similar idea to the forest families in my mom's children's books, but these were a different brand and style.

The figures and the treehouse were really cute, though, and I knew Victoria would use them to play "Garden City" with the figures.

"She already tried everything out," Justin said.

"Aw, she did? When?"

"A little while ago."

"I thought you were hanging out with Gretchen."

"I told you she left early. I went to the gym, and Mac and Victoria were outside when I got home, so I gave it to her."

"Aw, that's so cool. I'll bet she was so excited. I wish I was there to see her."

For the next hour, we talked. We talked about Victoria, and then Justin asked about my work. He took interest in a few of the athletes based on my past stories about them, and I updated him on how they had done this last week. We spoke so continually that I had no idea that it had turned midnight until my phone rang.

I heard it and I took it from my ear. "Oh, no," I said absentmindedly when I saw Heath's name.

"What?"

"Heath's calling in. I have to take it and explain something to him.

"Okay," Justin said.

He seemed slightly more reluctant about it than usual, and I said, "Is it okay?"

"Yeah, I said it was okay," he said, still sounding agitated. "It's not like I would tell you what calls you can take."

"I just have to clear something up with him," I said.

"It's fine," he said.

But it wasn't.

"Can I call you back?" I asked.

"Yes," he said. There was something serious and vulnerable to his voice and it caused me to experience a warm wave of feelings. I heard his voice in a new way, and I felt my heart begin to race.

"I'll call you back," I said.

Heath had already hung up by the time I got off of the phone with Justin. I called him back instantly. I didn't even give myself time to think about it. I listened to the phone ring, regretting that decision.

"Hey, where are you?" was the first thing he said when he picked up the phone.

"Hey, I meant to call you. I'm sorry I waited so late."

"Where are you? Are you coming up here?"

"No."

"Why not?"

I didn't know how to answer. I hadn't decided what I was going to say to him. "I, uh, I have… diarrhea," I said.

It was a thought that had crossed my mind when I was coming up with excuses earlier, so that's what came out of my mouth. I cringed.

"Huh?" he said, making a noise like he couldn't have possibly understood me.

"Yes," I said. "It's... bad."

"Uhh, okay," he said, this time with confusion and disgust.

"Yeah, I ate a chicken wrap on my way to the airport, and I knew it didn't taste right."

Silence.

"So, I, uh, guess I'll see you in the morning. With everyone else, for cherry blossoms and the movie."

"Yeah," he said, reluctantly.

"Unless you don't want me to come," I said, sensing his reluctance.

"Whatever. If you think you'll be feeling better by then," he said.

I sighed the most stomachache-ey sigh I could come up with. "Yeah, I should be okay in the morning, but I'll text you if something happens."

"Okay," he said, sounding frustrated.

He didn't say goodbye. I heard the sound of him hanging up as I was speaking. "Bye," I said, mostly to myself.

Chapter 7

I called Justin back the minute I hung up the phone with Heath. I was grinning nervously from ear to ear at the memory of what I said. I couldn't believe it. I tried to be calm, knowing that Justin was about to pick up.

"Hey," he said.

"Hey."

"That was fast."

"Yeah. It was really awkward, but I guess it was fast. It had that going for it."

"What happened?" Justin asked. "What made it awkward?"

"He just... I.... nothing."

"What?"

I breathed. "Nothing."

"Tell me," he said.

"We were hanging out all night with other people, and everything was fine and normal between us. We were just being casual, like always..."

"And then..." he said when I paused.

"And then, he had his friend give me a... the guy handed me a room key, and I sort of got the impression that he wanted me to go back to his room later. At midnight. You know, by myself or whatever."

Silence.

"Hello?" I said.

Justin cleared his throat. "Are you going to meet him?" he asked, sounding intentionally calm.

"No," I answered quickly.

"Are you and him, have you, do you, does he usually ask you things like that?"

"No," I said. "In fact, I don't even know what he's asking this time. Niall just handed me a room key and said I should go back up to Heath's room at midnight. He didn't specifically say what we were going to do."

"He didn't have to. It's midnight in a hotel, Katie. You're not going to be playing Yahtzee."

"Dang. I was planning on taking some dice up there, and a scorecard.

"I hope you're not going," he said.

"I'm not. I told him a lie. I made up some reason that I couldn't."

"You should just tell him that I asked you not to," he said. Again, he seemed serious, sincere.

I felt a wave of something warm at his protective tone. I tried to speak, but I stuttered. "D-did you ask me not to?" I asked.

"I don't think it's a good idea for you to go up to his room."

"Oh, because I thought you were saying it like you *personally* didn't want me to."

"I *don't* want you to," he said.

"Like you're jealous?" I asked, half joking.

"Yeah, like I'm jealous. If that's what keeps you from going to him tonight, then yes."

I wasn't quite sure what to make of that, so I closed my eyes and said nothing for a few seconds.

"Katie?"

"Yeah, I'm here," I said before clearing my throat and continuing. "I wasn't going up," I said. "I blew that opportunity and probably any other opportunity I have with Heath."

"What do you mean?"

"I told him I had a stomachache," I said. "A graphic stomachache."

"What's a graphic stomachache?"

"I was graphic with the details of my stomachache," I said. "My fake stomachache."

"What'd you tell him? You puked?"

"Diarrhea," I said.

Justin instantly busted out laughing. "You're kidding," he said.

"No, I'm not. I kind of wish I was," I said, laughing with him. "I'm actually pretty sure he never wants to see me again. No telling what he thought was going on with me.

"Yeah, diarrhea kind of ruins the moment," Justin agreed. "It's a full-proof excuse, for sure."

"Yeah, I was pretty proud of myself," I said.

We laughed, and we stayed in a laughing mood, talking for another hour before I let him go.

I set my alarm for the following morning, just so I could text Heath and tell him I would not be able to make it. I was supposed to meet him in the lobby at 9am, and I set the alarm for 8 to make sure I had enough time to wake up and decide what I was going to say to him.

For the sake of my own pride, I wanted to go with him. Even if I didn't end up being with Heath in the long run, I wanted him to think better of me than someone who has bathroom problems. I almost got dressed and went down there for no other reason than to have Heath see me alive and healthy.

I didn't though. I wasn't sure that I wanted to get to know him any further, anyway. We had fun together, but things were always pretty shallow between us.

I didn't mind that our relationship was over, but I couldn't believe what I had said. It was because of Justin that I did something so crazy. He was giving me feelings on the phone. He was saying things that made my stomach tie in knots with anticipation. If I hadn't been so wound up from being on the phone with Justin, I would have never said that to Heath.

I felt a little bit embarrassed about the way things had gone down with me and Heath, but I also knew he wasn't my destiny.

I wasn't planning on going downstairs that morning, but I had some things to work through before I sent the text. Ultimately, this was what I sent.

Me: Hey, sorry but I'm still not up for getting out today. I wish I could be there. Please tell Niall and the cast and crew I said congratulations. Thanks for looking me up when you came out West. I wish we could have hung out more. Maybe next time!

I wanted to let him down easy and also let myself down easy since he probably didn't want me there, anyway.

I didn't hear anything back from Heath.

My flight left Vancouver at 4:30 that afternoon, and I still hadn't heard back from him. I thought I might never hear from him again. It was a weird feeling after talking to someone for over a year, but part of me wasn't surprised that it ended so oddly and abruptly. I guess that was how breakups went— relationship endings were usually abrupt. *Was that what was going on here? Were Heath and I breaking up?* It hardly felt like a breakup since we weren't officially together. But we had been in each other's lives for long enough that there was a void.

I wasn't a shopper, but I went shopping in Canada before I left. I bought myself three outfits, a set of pajamas, some new panties and a bra, and even a new pair of shoes. I bought so many new things that I had to buy a duffle bag to get them all home.

I didn't do this very often, so I didn't give myself a hard time about it. They were all clothing items I didn't see back home, and most were bargains, so I got a little carried away. But it was therapeutic buying clothes. It made me feel like I was getting a fresh start.

I wore one of my new outfits on the plane. It was high-waisted shorts with a floral blouse. They were bright and summery and fit me well.

I knew my style but I never really learned what cut of clothing looked best on me or why. The girl at the store knew what she was doing, and she was the one who suggested the outfit I was wearing today. I felt confident and comfortable in it, and I was excited to get home and see everyone.

I called Justin on my way home. He said that everyone was at the house, making dinner. Ozzy and Justin were in charge of grilling hamburgers and hotdogs and the girls, Bri and Victoria, were making dessert.

They were being secretive about the dessert menu, and Justin wasn't sure what it was, but he said the house smelled like cookies.

It was right at 6pm when I got home.

Mac's house was huge, and I walked into the side door, through the front of the house and down a hallway to my room without anyone hearing or seeing me. I knew where they were. They were in the back kitchen—the one that led to the patio area. I could hear them back there.

I went to my room and set down my bags. I took a short look in the mirror before heading out to meet everyone else. I was coming down the hall when I saw Bri and Victoria walking toward me. Victoria loved me, and she began running the instant I smiled and held out my arms.

"You look so cute," Bri said to me as I picked up Victoria with a groan.

"I was just about to say the same thing about you two. How adorable."

"I got you one, too," Bri said. "I bought us all matching t-shirts for Victoria being such a big girl."

"Do I have one of these, too?" I asked with wide eyes, my question directed to Victoria.

She nodded, and my jaw dropped like I couldn't believe it. "I wanted to braid all of our hair later, but how will we be able to tell each other apart?"

I acted serious, and she giggled. "We *can* still," she said.

I leaned in and kissed her cheek. "I missed you."

"Where did you go?" she asked.

"To Canada."

"To Canada? Where's that?"

"It's a whole other country, but it's only an hour away by plane."

"You rode on a plane?"

"Yeah, just like your mom and Mac are doing right now"

"Is Canada where you got your shirt?" she asked, pulling back and staring at my chest. She was wearing a serious expression, and I couldn't tell if she liked it or not.

"Yes, it is," I said. "And these shoes and shorts," I said. "I brought you something, too."

"What is it?"

"It's something to go with your little playset Justin got you. It's a swing that hangs from a branch on the tree. I was thinking of those little bunnies— how cute they would look on a swing."

Victoria was a quiet little girl, but she made a silly but happy expression before pretending to pass out. I laughed and tickled her, which made her squirm. I set her on her feet.

She stared up at me. "Are you ready to put on your shirt?"

"Oh, she will," Bri said. "I'll get it for her in a few minutes. She looks so pretty in this one."

My hands were free for the first time, and Bri reached out for a hug. "Thank you," I said, hugging her back. "I'm excited about my Lalaloopsy t-shirt. I always knew we should be triplets."

We all started walking, heading toward the back of the house. Victoria stared down at her t-shirt, inspecting it after my statement.

We rounded the corner into the back kitchen and saw Justin standing at the other end of the room. He had on khaki shorts and a black t-shirt with the name of one of his sponsors on it. It was something about a rhino and I knew it had to do with customizing vehicles. I had seen him in several of those shirts before, but I never noticed the way they fit tightly across his chest.

Chapter 8

Justin

Justin was so busy tending to the grill that he forgot it was time for Katie to come home. He was aware that it was roughly time, but he was focused on the food, and he turned around and she was there.

He had just come in the door with a heavy pan of hot food, and he paused in his tracks when he saw her walk into the room with Bri and Victoria. She was wearing an outfit he had never seen her in before. Her shirt had little puffy shoulders and the shorts and shirt both fit snuggly around her waist, accentuating her hourglass figure.

Justin was balancing a cake pan that was full of burgers and hotdogs, and he almost dropped it. He greeted Katie as he went to set it on the counter.

"Hey, I just got here like one minute ago," Katie said, sounding casual and in a good mood. She smiled and took a deep sniff in through her nose, staring at the pan of meat.

"Oh, my goodness, it smells so good, and I'm starving."

She went right up to Justin, not acting shy at all. She hugged him, and he wrapped his arms around her waist to hug her back. He had hugged Katie hundreds of times since they met, but this time he didn't know how to do it properly. He didn't know how to let her go. He didn't want to let her go. He thought he might have done it too quickly to counteract this instinct.

"Can we get into this?" she asked, not paying attention. She was trying to get into the meat. She leaned over and stared into the pan.

"Yes, but careful, it's hot," Justin said.

"Well, look what the cat drug in," Ozzy said, coming in that same door, behind Justin.

"Hey, Oz, what's up. I came home at just the right time. It smells like dinner *and* dessert in here." Victoria tapped Katie's leg, and she looked down at the little girl.

"We made ice cream cookie casserole," Victoria said, quietly informing Katie.

Katie swooned like she might pass out from sheer pleasure. She looked like a model in those clothes, and yet she was acting silly and natural and making faces for a preschooler.

Victoria giggled at her.

"When can we eat?" Katie asked her, looking desperate.

"Right now!" Victoria said excitedly even though she didn't know.

"Look at those fancy shorts," Ozzy said, looking at Katie as he came farther into the kitchen.

"You like these?" she said, sticking out her mid-section in a pose."

"You big nerd," Ozzy said, smiling and shaking his head at her. "But yes, they look good. Where are you going?"

"Nowhere."

"I love those shorts, too," Bri said. "I might have to borrow them sometime."

"Anytime," Katie said.

"Can we seriously make plates?" Bri asked, looking at Justin. She came into the kitchen with the rest of them.

"Yeah, everything's ready," Justin said.

They all began to move around the kitchen, and Justin went to Victoria and put his hands out like he wanted to hold her. She was an easy-going little girl who went to him without hesitation.

"Do you want me to make you a hotdog or a hamburger?" Justin asked.

"I'll make her a plate," Katie said.

"I can do it," Justin said. "You make yourself one. You already said you were hungry."

Without warning, Katie took one big step and came to stand right next to Justin, completely crowding his space cuddling up to Victoria like she missed her so much. One second, she was not next to them, and then there she was, basically bumping into them.

She leaned into Victoria, who was taller than her since Justin was holding her up on his level. "I'm so happy you're hanging out with all of us this week!"

Katie said. She was casual and happy, and Victoria patted her shoulders.

"I'm so glad, too," Victoria said. "We will put those bunnies on a swing."

"Oh, thank goodness," Katie said.

Justin had no idea what they were talking about, and he didn't ask. He was too transfixed, anyway. He saw something different in Katie today, and it had nothing to do with her new outfit. He had kind of already figured out that he wanted her in a different way, but being next to her confirmed it.

They had been friends for a long time. Justin felt gratitude toward her. He was so thankful to Mac and his family for making his home life so pleasurable and easy. He felt unconditional support and love from them, and it contributed to the fact that he had a good season with the Seahawks. He was thankful for Katie's presence in his life, and he felt a bit like he had taken her for granted until now.

He had talked to her quite a bit on the phone last night. Neither of them had come out and said anything, but he felt that things were shifting between them. He wondered if she felt that, too. He thought she might. She stared at him for a few seconds… blinking.

"What?" he asked, since he could tell by her expression that he missed something. She had on this blue and white top that made the blue in her eyes look teal. Justin had always loved Katie's hazel eyes. He used to appreciate them in a disconnected way and marvel about how they could possibly be blue-green around the edges and brown in the center.

Now he looked at them, and he thought he sensed a changed expression. *Did he? Was she looking at him differently? Or was he just being hopeful? Why did he feel like he might lean down and kiss Katie?*

"Justin," she said.

"What?"

"I was telling you about the swing for the treehouse, and then Bri asked if you wanted a toasted bun or regular."

"Oh, toasted, please. Or regular. It doesn't matter."

He looked at Katie. "What's going on with a swing?"

"I got it for Victoria in Canada. There was a toy store when I was shopping today. It's a little thing that goes with the tree house."

And just like that, Katie broke away from them so she could focus on making a plate. She looked back at Justin.

"Are you sure you don't want me to make Victoria's?" she asked.

"I have Victoria's right here," Bri said. "I'm making hers and Justin's since he has his hands full."

"What? My hands are empty," he said.

He settled Victoria on his hip and let go of her strategically so she knew she had to hang on. She latched on to him, and he let go of her, demonstrating that his hands were completely clear before smiling and holding Victoria again. She laughed at that and leaned into Justin.

"I can seriously do that," Justin said to Bri.

But she just smiled and said, "I've got it. How was Canada?" she asked, turning to Katie.

"It was good," Katie said.

"Did you have fun with Heath?" Bri raised her eyebrows a few times suggestively.

"Yeah, I mean, we had fun like we always have." Katie's voice was slightly higher than usual. It was obvious that she was uncomfortable. She slumped a little. "Not really. I hoped to like it more. It was okay. He sent a guy to pick me up at the airport, and that all went smooth. The trip itself went smooth. We hung out in this big suite—like ten of us. I was supposed to go with them to breakfast and then to a screening of a movie, but I ended up skipping it and going shopping by myself."

"Whoa, was it weird between you two?" Bri asked.

"No, but it wasn't like it was just me and him hanging out. There were a lot of us, and it kind of got overwhelming. I canceled on them today and went shopping instead. There were some really cool stores in Vancouver. That's where I got these fancy shorts. And speaking of fancy shorts... I'd love to change my top. Where's my Lalaloopsy t-shirt?" She glanced at Bri. "If you've got Justin and Victoria's plate under control, I might as well go change into my party shirt."

"What could be more of a party shirt than what you have on?" Justin asked, feeling like he didn't want her to change.

Why did he care what she was wearing? He reminded himself that he didn't care.

"Bri got me a shirt to match the girls," Katie said, explaining to Justin.

Victoria got excited and stiffened out when she heard Katie was changing. Katie had already picked up a plate, but she set it down on the cabinet and said she would come back for it.

"It's in a black and white bag from the mall— either in the mudroom or in that entryway. I can't remember where I put it."

Katie smiled and nodded at Bri and took off while everyone else was busy making plates and talking about other things. Under normal circumstances, Justin would have forgotten all about Katie's absence in the room and moved on, seeing to Victoria and to Bri and the plates she was making. But he felt differently tonight. Tonight, he wanted to follow Katie. He wanted a moment alone with her.

Justin had always been the type of guy who took action when he decided he wanted something. He wasn't sure exactly what he wanted, but he knew it was no longer in the room.

"I'm going to set you right here for a second," he said to Victoria, settling her on the counter next to

Bri who was making her plate. "I'm going to use the restroom. You don't have to make me one," he said to Bri.

She looked at him. "I don't mind doing it. I'm already going on it. I'll just make you a burger like mine, if you want."

"That's fine," he said. "But you don't have to. Just so you set Miss Victoria up with a hotdog and extra mustard. Lots and lots of mustard."

"Noooo," Victoria said, smiling at him for messing up her order on purpose.

"Extra horseradish," he said, snapping his fingers like he was trying to remember.

"Noo-oo-oo," she said, laughing.

"Okay, extra ketchup," he said, and she nodded and settled down as he walked away.

They thought he was using the restroom, but he was only in search of Katie. He went straight for the part of the house where Bri told Katie she could find the shirt. He walked quickly, smiling at himself for the fact that he was tempted to jog.

Justin rounded the corner into the mudroom, and he heard Katie let out a little shriek of surprise when she saw him come in.

"Oh, hey, you almost caught me changing," she said.

She was on the far end of the mud room, standing in front of a full-length mirror, straightening her shirt. She went back to looking at her reflection when she saw that it was Justin.

He walked toward her, knowing that he was going to offer her no explanation whatsoever before he tried to kiss her. She was wearing a cartoon shirt that matched the other two girls. "It covers up my shorts, but I didn't want to tuck it in because you wouldn't be able to see the—" Katie stopped talking mid-sentence, turning with a curious expression when she saw Justin coming toward her with intention.

He pulled her into his arms, taking a hold of her. He leaned down, looking at her, aiming his mouth for hers, letting his lips touch hers.

He.

Kissed.

Her.

Ohhhh.

Yep.

His lips settled on hers, and it was as good as he imagined.

He kissed Katie softly three or four times.

He had been around her constantly for the last year. *How had this never happened?*

He pulled back just far enough to apologize to her.

"What for?" she whispered when he did.

And he took that as permission to do it again. Only this time, he opened his mouth, coaxing her to do the same. Katie leaned into him, willingly opening, pulling, drawing him closer.

Justin never dreamed he would react this way to her. He knew at the very first taste of her that he never wanted to kiss anyone else for the rest of his life. She was the best thing he would ever find.

He held Katie, gripping her and kissing her deeply for several long seconds. He felt her and tasted her, and his fingertips and whole body were alive with some kind of new excitement he hadn't felt before. She lit him on fire. He was burning hot. Katie was delicate and soft and warm, and yet she kissed him like she was just as eager as he was.

Then suddenly, she pulled back, looking at him with a stunned expression. "Shhhh. Somebody's comi—oh, my goodness, go, Justin!" She had been whispering, but she suddenly shoved at him, forcing him away. Justin was completely out-of-it, but he went toward the door.

"Oh, hey Justin. I was yelling for you. Do you want tomatoes on your burger?"

Bri had no clue. She had just barged in on what might have been the most magical moment of Justin's life, and she was smiling and talking about dad-blasted tomatoes.

"Yeah, it doesn't matter," Justin said, feeling like he might explode.

"Hey were you guys looking for me?" Katie said, coming up from behind Justin and looking like

76

she didn't just see him and she didn't just get utterly crushed by his kiss.

"I was asking Justin what he wanted on his burger," Bri said. "And I can make you one, too, if you want. Oh, that shirt's so cute on you!" Bri added, pulling back to look at Katie.

"We'll have to get a picture of all three of us," Katie said. She brushed past Justin nonchalantly, locking arms with Bri as they headed toward the kitchen.

"Did you want tomatoes on your burger?" Katie asked, turning to glance at Justin from over her shoulder as they all walked.

Bri stayed facing forward so she could lead them, and Katie shared a conspiratorial glance with Justin behind Bri's back. Her eyes widened, and Justin's chin nudged forward as he made a face of brutish discontent at the fact that they had been interrupted. She smiled at him for doing that, and then she turned to walk with Bri.

"Yeah, sure, I'll have a tomato," Justin said from behind them.

Chapter 9

Katie

I tried my best to remain calm and pretend nothing had happened, but Justin Teague, one of my very best friends in the whole world, had just kissed the living daylights out of me.

I was already feeling a little gut-tingly toward him when I got home, so I didn't hesitate to go to him when he crossed that laundry room headed toward me, looking like he was about to devour me.

I got chills at the memory of it, and I did my best not to physically shiver. I was arm-in-arm with Bri, and we walked down the hall, toward the kitchen where Ozzy was watching Victoria who was already working on her hotdog.

I took it all in, trying to look around and be present in the moment so that no one would know what just happened. I was shaking, and I squeezed Bri's arm so that she wouldn't notice.

"Look at KK's shirt!" Bri announced.

Victoria made an excited face at me.

"Everything seriously smells so good in here," I said. "I can't wait to eat some of this hamburger!"

I wasn't hungry at all.

It was an act.

All I could pay attention to was the buzzing in my chest. *Hamburger, hamburger, hamburger. Just be calm and make yourself a dang hamburger, Katherine.* I said those words in my mind as I headed toward the kitchen.

"Your burger is right here, Justin," Bri said.

"I just need to put the tomato on it."

She let go of me and jogged to the spot where she had been making Justin's plate. She finished the burger with a tomato before putting on the top bun. I had come to stand in the kitchen by this point, and I watched as Bri turned and handed the plate to Justin with a smile. He reached out for it, and in that moment, I felt a stab of jealousy. *Was it normal for Bri to make Justin a plate of food?* I thought it was, but it felt wrong.

She smiled and he smiled, and it all seemed like something they would do every day, but I wasn't sure I liked it. I had made Justin plates of food lots of times before and it didn't mean anything. I reminded myself of this. He had made plates for all of us. We were a plate-making crew—a share-everything type of crew. I tried to reassure myself of this when Justin took the plate of food from Bri and I felt jealous and protective.

I went through the motions of making a burger. I even ate most of it in spite of being distracted and not hungry. I talked with everyone, keeping up with the conversation and making jokes like I always did. But there was a second conversation going on in my subconscious. I kept noticing Justin. I noticed everything about him. I noticed his jaw, and his nose, and his arms, and his hands. I noticed his hair, and his mouth, and his knees, and his feet. I could not stop noticing Justin. I made the effort to look at everyone equally when we were talking, but the world stopped when I looked at Justin.

Every time our eyes met, he would give me a knowing smile, which made my body have all sorts of reactions. I had to look away when he smiled at me. I was all worked up by Justin, and all I could do was be normal and act like that wasn't the case.

It hadn't fully sunk in that he had kissed me in the back room. I knew it had happened, but it still didn't seem real. I thought I might have hallucinated the whole thing, and I kept doubting the reality of it. But then our eyes would meet as we were all talking and eating, and not only was it real, but I felt like there was a good chance that it was going to happen again.

There was no way we could let any of this be known in front of the others, though. It was just too weird to think about Justin and I liking each other romantically. The family wasn't ready for that— especially not on a weekend where we were babysitting.

I kept the conversation casual, trying to act like I would always act and not care at all whether or not Justin kissed me. I also tried not to care that Bri made Justin a plate of food, or that she sat next to him while we were eating.

The four of us were overeager babysitters. We had all sorts of tricks up our sleeves with games, toys, and time-wasting ideas. But Victoria had an easygoing personality, and she seemed comfortable with the fact that Mac and Morgan weren't there. She was content to hang out and entertain herself like she always did.

We were overstaffed that evening with caretakers, and Ozzy was the first to excuse himself after dinner to work on a project he was doing for school. The rest of us made a spot in the living room where we would have a movie night. Bri had lines to memorize for a play she was doing at school but she decided she could stay up late to do it so that she could watch a movie with us.

Victoria got to choose, so we watched Nacho Libre. It was a Jack Black movie that wasn't necessarily meant for toddlers but was one of Victoria's favorites. She had seen it at least a dozen times. There were four of us left at the party after Ozzy went to his room, and we all piled onto the couch. We had already eaten burgers and hot dogs, but that didn't stop us from making bowls with chips, popcorn, and candy.

We all sat on the couch at first, watching the movie and passing around bowls of snacks. We tried to talk a little, but Victoria was such a fan of the movie, that she would tap us and get our attention to make sure we were watching. We shared several glances with each other when she kept us in line about Nacho.

With the way our seating arrangements had played out, I could see Justin, but there was no way we would come into contact physically. For one, Victoria was between us. And also, there was too much space. The couch was huge and L-shaped, and there was enough room for us all to sprawl out and no reason for us to invade each other's space or touch each other at all.

It was really too bad because my heart was being tugged to Justin. I physically wanted to be next to him.

The movie was over halfway done when I felt something move in the couch behind me. I could see Victoria in front of me, and knew it wasn't her, my first thought, honestly, was that there was a mouse or some other kind of varmint crawling in the couch.

I let out an instinctual little yelp, and everyone looked at me at the exact same time. It was then that I figured out that it was Justin's hand that had been moving. He had shifted far enough toward me on the couch that his hand was reaching behind pillows to touch me.

"I thought I felt something behind me but it was nothing," I said, explaining the noise. I had a bowl of M&M's in my hand, and I casually took one more bite of candy to make things look natural. Then I reached forward and set down the bowl.

"What did you feel?" Bri asked.

"I have no idea. Probably my imagination."

"He's about to say *he's going to buy a bus for the orphans*," Victoria said. She was serious about her Nacho Libre, and she had to keep us focused on the movie. In this moment, I appreciated that very much.

I glanced at Justin and saw that he was smiling. He was looking at the television, but he saw me look at him in his periphery, and an amused grin covered his face that had nothing to do with the movie. He was sprawled out on the couch and it wasn't obvious at all that he had his hand all the way behind me, but I knew he did. I knew what I felt.

I sat back on the couch. I didn't want to make it obvious, but I did my best to sit back far enough so that it could happen again.

I was out-of-practice at these types of moves. I didn't know how to hold hands with someone anymore—especially without getting caught. *Was that even what was going on here?* I almost got bold and stuck my hand behind the pillow to find out. But I didn't. I curled up on the couch with my knees to one side, pretending like I was getting comfortable to finish the movie and had nothing else on my mind.

Justin's hand found me right away.

Goodness gracious. My body was flooded with a warm rushing feeling the instant he touched me. *What in the world had happened to me?* This was Justin. I had literally sat on this exact couch and watched this exact movie five other times with this man. *So, what was different this time?* I wanted his touch so badly that it frightened me.

I took a deep breath, trying to calm my racing heart and decide how I was going to react to the feeling of electricity in the place where his hand was touching my arm.

I stared at the screen, not taking in the movie at all. I stayed still for another minute, letting myself catch my breath. I concentrated on not shaking.

I readjusted at a time and in a way that seemed natural. I cocked my feet out, away from Justin and toward Bri, adjusting myself on the pillow where my hand and arm were behind it. It took him a minute to find me again, but I was closer to him now. I felt his arm move slowly until it reached mine. At first, his hand was on my forearm, but he slowly pulled back until our hands connected.

This was not at all what it usually felt like when I touched Justin.

I glanced at him, and he stared back at me. Our eyes locked, and our gazes held. He was staring directly at me with those blue eyes and unapologetically holding my hand.

It was like a dream. No offense to myself, because I truly did love myself and know that God loved me, too, but Justin was out of my league.

I knew it, and that was why it had been so easy being friends with him and nothing more.

Gretchen was a blonde bombshell—the kind of girl who wore a bathing suit any chance she got. She took a few vacations a year and she always went somewhere tropical. If you gave me a few seconds, I could find about twenty photos of her in swimsuits on her social media.

I knew a lot of professional athletes, and the good majority of them had wives who looked amazing in bikinis. Gretchen was such a cookie cutter athlete wife that I tried to set her up with my brother before I set her up with Justin. I had no idea why I had done that. My stomach flipped at the thought of it. Or perhaps I was just feeling that way because Justin was holding my hand behind the pillows.

His hand was big and warm, and it was callused from so much football. Handoffs from the quarterback were always rushed and often rough, and Justin had big, strong hands that were capable of dealing with constant abuse. I felt his thumb absentmindedly run across the back of my hand, and I thought I might melt.

I wanted to go to him. I wanted to hug him and have him hold me back. I realized that I didn't care about Gretchen or feel threatened that I wasn't like her. Justin had kissed me and now he was fishing his arm through a bunch of pillows just so he could hold my hand in secret.

He liked me. I could tell by the way he was holding onto me that he liked me.

Chapter 10

Justin

"I'm going to do Victoria's nighttime routine," Katie said, getting off of the couch as soon as the credits started rolling.

She was holding his hand one minute, and then just like that, she let go, getting off of the couch and stretching before looking down at Victoria.

"Did you see it when he flew off the side and then... whoosh!" Victoria made a noise and a gliding motion with her hand, demonstrating Nacho's flight pattern. The girl truly did love that movie.

Justin didn't move from his spot on the couch, but he looked up, watching Victoria and Katie as they interacted.

"That was great," Bri said, standing up on the other side of the couch. Justin could barely see her with the way he was tucked into the corner behind a pillow. "I hadn't ever seen it the whole way through," Bri added.

Katie made a gasping noise. "What? Are you serious? How?" Katie asked the questions in such an exaggerated tone that it was obvious she was pushing Victoria's buttons. Victoria made a face at Bri like she couldn't believe it, and they all laughed.

"I don't know," Bri said. "I see you playing it all the time, but I've never sat down and watched it. I've seen pieces of it, though. It was good. Did you like it Justin? Is he awake?"

Justin would normally have sat up or even stood by this point, but he wasn't ready to leave the house just yet.

He propped up from behind his pillow, smiling at Bri. "I did enjoy it," he said. "I enjoyed it a lot, actually. It's about my fifth time to see it, but I loved it the most this time. It's one of my favorite movies ever now."

Victoria giggled with delight over that. "Did you see it when he blew the chips?" she asked.

"I did," Justin said, nodding and smiling at her. "Do you mean at the beginning?"

She nodded and smiled.

"Well, it's almost ten o'clock, so I'm going to get little miss beautiful to bed," Katie said. She looked at Justin. "What are you guys going to do?" She asked the question like she was talking to both of them, so she glanced at Bri who smiled and shrugged.

"Are you going to hang out over here a little while longer?" Bri asked Justin.

"Probably so," he said.

"Okay, I'll be twenty or thirty minutes with Victoria," Katie said, informing them. "I'll come back out in a little bit and see if you guys are still here. If not, I'll see you tomorrow."

She was so easygoing about it, that Justin thought she might actually not care if he was there when she came out.

"Kay, night, Victoria," Bri said. "Sleep good."

"Night," Victoria said.

"Love you," Bri said.

"Love you," Victoria answered. "Love you Uncle J," she added.

"Love you, little Nacho."

Victoria giggled at him as she followed Katie out of the room. Justin's eyes met Katie's just before she walked away. She stared straight at him. He had no idea what she was thinking, but he thought she wanted him to stay. He swore he could see that in her eyes in spite of how casual she was being in front of Bri. He was staying either way. Katie had kissed him back, and she had held his hand. Her delicate hand. Her fingers were cold at first, and Justin remembered how small and soft her hands felt in his.

Katie.

KK.

She was funny and kind, and he trusted her wholeheartedly. She already took on the job of helping him organize and maintain his personal life. She was smart, and she was such a trusted friend that she had a hand in the function of Justin's everyday life. She was a natural organizer, a streamliner, and she had given him advice on everything from contracts and sponsorships to even more personal things like finances, daily scheduling, and social media. She had helped him figure out a more efficient way to do part of his off-season workout routine at home, which saved him three hours of commuting a week.

Katie had been there for Justin in countless ways since he moved to Seattle. He felt gratitude toward her. In his thoughts about Katie, he felt thankful, comfortable, and content. The feelings only intensified as he watched her scoop up Victoria and walk away with the girl on her hip. He loved that she was the one who was doing that. She was good at everything.

Justin stayed on the couch for the next twenty minutes, waiting for her. Bri went to the kitchen for a minute but came back right away. They talked about her school. She was just finishing up her junior year of college. She was majoring in something normal like Accounting, but she minored in Theater, and most of her school conversations were about whatever production they were currently working on. This time, it was Mama Mia.

Justin wasn't nearly as lazy as he was letting on. He wasn't normally a *lie on the couch for hours and watch one movie after another* type of guy, so this was unusual for him.

"I don't mind hanging out for another movie if Katie gets back," he said. "Or at least part of one."

Bri nodded and shrugged. "I could use the time to study some lines, but it can wait till later, or even tomorrow morning."

"All right," he said.

He sat up and tossed the remote her way. "Maybe you could find something for us to watch while I go use the restroom."

Justin had to go one way to reach Victoria's bedroom and another way to reach Katie's. He wasn't sure which side of the house to choose. Katie had mentioned that she was thinking about where to have Victoria sleep when Mac and Morgan were out of town, but he didn't know what she decided.

He went toward Mac and Morgan's side of the house, and he smiled when he saw the bedroom door cracked and the low light coming from Victoria's room. He knew they were inside, and he smiled as he approached the door. He was hoping Katie would come out soon so they could have a few seconds alone before they went back out there with Bri. His plan was to peek into Victoria's bedroom and check on them. He was going to try to do it without disturbing the girl.

He went to glance into the door, but he stopped short when he heard Katie talking.

"… and he said, *'why in the world does this taste so good?'* and the bear said, *'because all the honey fell into it,'* and after that, they had a new, popular menu item, and they all lived happily ever after."

Justin smiled, knowing he made it just in time for the end of the story.

"We could do another one," Victoria said.

"We could, punkin', but I promised your mama I'd get you to bed on time. And I can see how sleepy you are. I would be sleepy, too, if I were you. You had a big day. Popcorn, Nacho Libre, hotdogs."

"We forgot to play with my new swing," Victoria said.

"Yeah, you're right, goodness. Let's say thanks for all that, okay, before you fall asleep, okay? Father in heaven, we thank you so much for popcorn, and movies, and hotdogs. We thank you for new toys that we haven't even opened yet, and for matching Lalaloopsy shirts, and for lots of good family and friends. Help us to be good people. Help us to show Your love to everyone around us. Please comfort those who are hurting, or sad, or who are too cold, or hot, or hungry. Thank You that we're not any of those things. Thank You that we're so comfortable. Thank You for Victoria. May she know how special, beautiful, and wonderful she is. Give her lots of gifts and talents, Lord, and teach her how to use them. Use Victoria in great ways, Father. Bless her life. Bless her rest. Thank You for helping us all rest well tonight. Help her mom and Mac to have fun on their trip and may we have fun while we're here waiting on them. Help Uncle Ozzy with his pictures. May he edit fast and have fun. Help Aunt Bri remember all her lines at the play, and let her get through this semester of accounting. And Uncle J, Lord. Justin, You know all the prayers I have about Justin. Help him in his work. Help his leg to feel better. Help him and Mac to both have strong, capable, agile bodies. Give them stamina and strength and success at football. Help them to..." She paused before continuing. "Anyyyywayyyy, I... I actually don't even need to finish, do I? I could say anything I want to say right now because this little angel is all-the-way a-sleep. Or maybe she's faking, and she is actually... (another pause) no, I guess you are asleep, huh, punkin'. Can you seriously fall asleep that fast? (another pause) Wow. Well, amen, Lord, and I love you, little sweet pea."

What was the matter with him tonight? He was stunned by Katie. It was a simple prayer, and it was more attractive to him than anything any other woman had ever done in his presence. Ever. That prayer had him so hooked on Katie, it was unbelievable. It was odd, even to Justin, that he could be attracted to someone for such a thing but he had to be with the person who prayed like that. He was dying to hear her do that again. He wanted to know what she was talking about when she said 'the prayers she had about Justin'.

He was so transfixed by her words that he forgot to expect that Katie would be coming out of the bedroom.

"Oh, my goodness I didn't see you," she said, trying her best to be quiet even though Justin startled her in the hallway. She was smiling at him, and he reached out and grabbed her arm, pulling her toward him, into his grasp.

"Kaaa-tie," Justin said her name hoarsely and with about as much need and desire as you could spill into one word.

"What are you doing?" she asked, smiling and looking down the hall like she was scared they might get caught in this compromised position. Justin didn't care if anyone was coming. He was not about to let her go.

"I was listening to you," he said.

"I see that," she said, letting out a laugh. "And I'm embarrassed. For how long? Did you hear that whole story and everything?"

"I missed that. I've only been here for about a minute."

Justin leaned down and smelled her neck, but he felt like he had to reign it in. He wanted to take her, kiss her, claim her again. He wanted to make sure she knew how much he wanted her. He just stood still, his arms gently around her, concentrating on being motionless.

"You're such a… good girl," he said, searching for the right words, and unable to come up with them. All night he had been wanting to hold her like this.

She made a little face at him. "A good girl? I'm not sure if that's a compliment, but thank you, I guess."

"You really have no idea what a compliment it is," Justin said.

Chapter 11

Katie

Justin kissed me in the hallway that night.

He was insatiable.

Some sort of flame had been ignited within him, and he was looking at me differently, like he was attracted to me. He kissed me twice that first evening, but I told him, after we almost got caught, that we had to pull back. I loved it, obviously, and I wanted to be close to Justin, but I told him we had to slow down and not be reckless with our friendship.

We were together a lot in the next few days, but we didn't kiss again or make any sort of physical contact. Our gazes held more than they used to, and our conversations seemed to go deeper, but we kept ourselves from being physical.

We had a lot going on, anyway. Mac had us working on a surprise while he and Morgan were out of town. They got a huge painting as a wedding gift from our Aunt Tess, and Morgan had been talking about how she wanted to paint the dining room blue to go with it. So, Mac had it done while they were gone. I had my days off of work, but I stayed busy dealing with that and watching after Victoria.

Ozzy and Bri both helped out, but they had things going on with school, so Victoria and I spent a lot of time with Justin. He and I went through the weekend and early part of the week trying to be as normal as possible. Most of the time, we were doing our best to not get caught looking at each other. We held hands a few times when it could truly be secret, but Victoria was with me all the time, and Justin and I did kid things with her and didn't give in to our attraction. We had plenty of private moments when Victoria was sleeping and Bri and Ozzy were busy, but we intentionally kept some distance.

So, Justin and I hadn't kissed or made much contact since that first night, and it was now Thursday and I had gone back to school and my normal routine.

Mac and Morgan got back at noon, and Bri had charge of Victoria during the morning while I was at work. She had planned on doing that and didn't mind at all. It was weird, though, being with Victoria all weekend and half the week and then not being at home when she went back to her mom.

I came home as quickly as I could, but I had work to catch up on, so it was 4pm by the time I arrived.

Bri and Justin were in the living room with Mac, Morgan, and Victoria when I walked in.

"Hey," I said, taking in the scene.

I had already been home for a minute and set down all of my things before I ever made it to the living room.

I wasn't used to being off duty with Victoria, and my eyes instantly found her. She was busy playing with some sort of ribbon tied to a stick that I assumed was a souvenir from their trip.

I went to Mac and Morgan to give them hugs, but I spoke to Victoria on my way over there. "I love your ribbon dancer," I said to her.

She didn't say anything but her moves got more exaggerated as she displayed her toy for me in its full glory. I beamed excitedly at her as I leaned in and hugged my brother. He squeezed me tightly, making me groan.

I was pressed against my brother's chest, and Justin was in my line of vision so I made eye contact with him. He was staring straight at me, and I realized that I was so much closer to him now than I was the last time I had seen my brother. Basically, Mac went away, and Justin and I fell in love.

I looked away from Justin when that hit me. I played it off, moving, turning, walking, going to hug Morgan.

"Thank you for taking such good care of her," Morgan said as we embraced.

"My pleasure. Our pleasure. She was so good, and Bri and Justin and Ozzy were here. It was a piece of cake."

"That's funny you say that because that's exactly what we were doing when they came home earlier."

It was Bri who had spoken and I looked at her.

"Did y'all make that cake mix this morning?" I asked. I knew she mentioned doing that with Victoria while I was at work.

"Yeah," Morgan said, answering for her. "I walked in to the three of them covered in flour and batter. It was the cutest thing. Ozzy got a picture, you'll have to see it."

"We had a cupcake fight," Bri said in silly, playful tones.

"Not a full fight," Justin said. "We basically just carefully dabbed stuff onto each other." Justin made a flicking motion with his fingers, displaying how gentle they had been.

"Yeah, no, they didn't make a big mess in the kitchen or anything," Morgan said.

"Unless they had already cleaned it up by the time we got here," Mac said, looking around.

"We made a little one," Justin said laughing.

"It was cute," Morgan said. "And the cupcakes actually tasted really good. I had two of them and I don't know how many Mac ate."

Victoria was still playing with her ribbon, but she laughed at that.

"There's more in the fridge if you want one," Bri said. "We saved you some."

"Thank you," I said, crossing to the refrigerator and search for something to drink.

"They're on the second shelf," Bri said, assuming that I was a going for a cupcake.

I was slightly jealous that they got made without me—and especially that there had been some sort of shenanigans with a food fight. But I went ahead and grabbed one.

"How was work?" Mac asked me. "I thought you had to go to a game tonight."

"I do, but I came home to say hey to y'all. I'll change and eat dinner and stuff, and then I'll go back. I think Justin was thinking about riding down there with me."

"Oh really?" Mac asked. He looked surprised, and Morgan nodded.

"Yeah, I thought you didn't tell your students you were friends with Justin," she said. "What kind of game are you seeing?"

"Girls softball," I said. "And I warned him, all those girls know who he is. They're all going to freak out when he goes over there."

"You ready to have all those high school girls swoon over you, J?" Mac asked, giving him a hard time.

"I'm only going to hang out with Katie," Justin said, shrugging with quiet confidence. It was an innocent enough comment, but he was looking at me when he said it, and it made my heart race.

"He's been asking me to go to a game since I started working there," I said.

"Yeah, and she always tells me she has a strict policy against it."

"I do have one," I said. "But Justin was the best this week, so—"

"So, he gets let out of the house to go to a softball game?" Mac said, teasing us both.

"I heard Justin helped out with Victoria," Morgan said.

"Oh, big time," Bri said. "He took care of most of the meals. He had a chef deliver us food a few times, and a few times, he cooked."

"You cooked Justin?" Morgan asked, looking surprised.

"Like three or four different meals," I said.

"One time he made avocado toast for lunch with this fancy bread with seeds all in it," Bri added.

"Yeah, Victoria loved that," Justin said. "She was all about the avocado toast."

I had poured myself a glass of water from the filter on the fridge, and I drank a sip of it while Bri asked Justin something about the cupcakes. He responded to her.

"Yeah, Lemon zest," she said. "We made that strawberry icing, and Justin thought of adding lemon zest. That's why it tastes citrusy. I didn't even know what 'zest' was. I thought he meant that I should just squeeze a little lemon into the icing, like 'zest' was the word for a pinch of lemon juice—a unit of measurement." She laughed and acted like she was squeezing an imaginary lemon in the air. "Like a zest of lemon," she said, performing a quick squeeze.

We laughed with Bri about that, which led to Morgan telling a story about a fancy dessert they had in Hawaii.

That led to me telling a story about a lady who has worked in the school cafeteria for so long that they recently named it after her. Our school cafeteria was now named Winnie's, complete with a sign and everything.

Winnie was funny. A lot of times, she was perfectly stone-faced, being strict with the kids, but she was self-aware, and she knew what she was doing and how they saw her. She was a character, and I imitated her as part of the story, which made everyone laugh. I had seen Henry Young imitating her, and it was hilarious, so I used some of his antics for my story. It was a hit, and Mac got in the action even though he had never met her. We made up a few things that she might say, and we all had a good laugh about it.

I was in the kitchen with everybody for a half hour or so before I excused myself. "I need to go change for the game," I said.

"All right, I'm going home, too," Justin said. "Just come by and get me when you're ready to go."

I glanced at him with a nod. "Ten minutes sound okay?"

Justin nodded back at me, and we both went our separate ways.

***

"It feels so weird not having to be aware of where Victoria is all the time," I said, twenty minutes later when Justin and I were on the road heading for Riverbend High School.

He had a really nice truck that was customized and got attention, so we drove my car. Justin was driving, and he had the seat pushed all the way back, looking like he was too big for it.

"Do you miss her?" he asked as he drove.

"I miss *her*, but I don't miss being in charge of her," I said, joking and laughing a little. "I do love Victoria, and I also want to be a mom myself. But I feel relieved in this moment. It's different with someone else's kid. I just kept being nervous that something was going to come up that I didn't know how to handle. Like, she'd choke or fall." I paused and smiled at him. "I'll tell you what, though, that little girl is easy. She's easy to take care of and easy to love. To answer your question, though, I feel a little relieved that I no longer have to keep someone else's kid alive, but, yes, I also miss her. She's a pumpkin."

"She is a pumpkin," he said.

We were at a stoplight when Justin's phone dinged and he picked it up and turned it over. He opened the screen, looked at it for a second and then handed it to me.

"It's Bri," he said. "It looks like that picture. Can you see what it is?"

Justin handed it to me so that he could continue driving. I opened the text. It was the picture of Justin, Victoria, and Bri. They had batter and flour on their faces, and it was framed just right with kitchen tools in the foreground. It was actually adorable. I smiled even though I was insanely jealous.

"She sent that picture of you guys," I said, sounding as happy as I could. "She's asking about it. She wants to know if you mind if she posts it on her Instagram."

We all appeared in each other's social media from time to time, but we always asked first, and we always said 'yes'. Of course, Justin was going to agree to it. There was no reason he shouldn't. It's not like we would say 'don't do it because Katie doesn't want you to' and he also wouldn't say 'don't do it because I don't want you to'. There was nothing we could say but 'yes'.

"I guess just text back and tell her 'yes', right? Is she waiting for an answer?"

Justin glanced at me, and I nodded. "Yes."

"Just tell her she can post it, I guess, unless you don't want her to."

"No, it's not like I would ever tell her that I don't want her to," I said.

"But do you want her to?"

"No, I don't want her to. I hate that photo. It's way too adorable."

"Are you jealous, Katie Klein?"

"I'm actually.... a little dang... jealous," I spoke it in a high-pitched tone, and he laughed and reached over to grab my hand as he drove.

"I want you to be jealous," he said, pulling my hand into his lap, holding onto me. My body had a warm reaction to him. He held onto me in a more impatient way than usual, and my heart pounded because of it.

"I'm happy if you're jealous," he said. "It's about time you're jealous."

"I'm still not going to tell Bri to keep that ridiculously good, piece of junk, freakin' lemon-zest picture of y'all off the internet." I was shaking my head, acting mad, acting silly but dramatic, and Justin smiled like he enjoyed me getting all bent out of shape about it.

"You could just text her back and tell her you're jealous and you don't want her to post it."

"I would never," I said.

"Then tell her to post it," he said.

"I will when you give me my hand back," I said.

"You can type with one hand," he said. He had a hold of my left hand and he wasn't letting go. The road was open, and as he drove, he turned my hand over and placed my palm on his cheek. I touched the stubble of his facial hair, and it made me feel all stirred up in the pit of my stomach. I fought the urge to curl forward, bracing myself against the crippling butterflies. It was honestly more than I could handle. "Goodness, Justin." I said, fussing at him.

"What?" he asked innocently.

"Why are you trying to make me touch your face?"

"Why not?" he said.

"Because it causes all sorts of problems for me."

"What kind of problems?" he asked. He held my hand so securely to his face I could feel his jaw move when he spoke.

"That right there," I said. "Holding your hand on my face. It makes my stomach feel really funny."

He laughed. "You mean holding *your* hand on *my* face?" Justin asked.

"That's what I said."

He made an expression like he was a little confused. "Yeah, but you… never mind. I get what you mean."

"Yeah. I don't even know what I'm saying. All I know is that your face is right there and my hand is on it, and it makes my stomach feel funny."

"Good," he said. "I'm trying to make your stomach feel funny."

I stared at him for a few perfect seconds, and in those seconds, I imagined a life with Justin. I got the warm fuzzy feeling of experiencing everything with him and then being old together.

I pulled my hand back when I realized I was getting way too carried away.

Chapter 12

"We're basically here," I said, explaining the fake reason why I took my hand away in the car. "We'll start passing kids and parents on this road."

"Nobody's looking at us," he said.

"Yeah, well, also, I told you, that was making me feel... my heart was going really fast, and..." I let out a breath. "Uhhh. We need to be friends in front of all these students, Justin. They notice *everything*, and they're already going to be freaking out enough to see you."

"Are you always going to have an excuse?" he asked.

"What do you mean?"

"Are we just going to be friends for the rest of our lives?"

"Well, I hope so," I said, taking his question the wrong way.

"You know what I mean," he said, not joking.

His tone made me nervous and I stuttered. "W-well, no, no, I'm, of course, Justin. It's just that these kids... like I said, they notice everything. If they think you're here with me, or whatever, it's not like they're going to just let it go. They'll say something. They'll call us out, ask us about it. Not only that, but they'd ask me for updates about it for the rest of my life. They're already going to be bugging me to bring you to all the games once they see us—J, what are you doing?"

"I'm holding your hand," he said.

"We're here," I said. "Just pull in right there. That's the field, down there on the left."

Justin knew I was reluctant, but he didn't let go of my hand, and I didn't argue any more. I wanted it to happen.

He looked at me from over the car when we got out. "I thought once Mac and Morgan got back and you weren't stressed about babysitting, you would just be able to be my girlfriend after that."

I widened my eyes at him because he was speaking at a normal volume and someone had parked near us. He just smiled at me like I was overreacting. I motioned for him to be quiet.

"They're not just going to see us making contact and forget about it," I said in a low tone. "They'll beg me to bring you around all the time. It's best if we act like we only kind of know each other. We can just say that we know each other through Mac, because they know my brother plays with you."

"Oh, so I'm just Mac's friend now and not your friend?" he asked, smiling at me and pretending he was injured even though he was the most confident person I knew.

"Can you please pop the trunk so I can get my chairs out of it?" I said. I was experiencing so many different emotions that I didn't know what to say.

Justin stooped over to pull the lever and pop my trunk before closing the car door and walking to the back of my car. We met at the trunk.

"I'm doing this for your sake," I said speaking quietly to him. "I'm trying to make it to where you have some privacy with these kids and they're not asking to see you all the time."

"Oh, oh, so you were just doing all this for me?"

I smiled at him as we closed the trunk. "Hey, Mrs. Martin," I said, waving at one of the student's mothers who was walking right behind us.

"Hello, Miss Klein, I see you brought a friend with you. Cody, my husband, would *lose his mind* if he knew I was staring Justin Teague in the face. We've been Hawks fans our whole lives. I'm so sorry, but do you mind if I just give you a hug?" But she wasn't planning on not hugging him. Even as she spoke, she moved toward Justin, not really giving him any other choice but to catch her. She squeezed him. "What a season, there, number twenty-two, my gosh. My goodness. I never in my wildest dreams thought I'd have my arms around Justin Teague. A thousand yards rushed? Are you some kind of machine? You *feel* like a machine," she said, pulling back and squeezing his arms, testing the actual feel of his back and shoulders. "Wow, this has made my day, thank you so much."

"Thanks for supporting us," Justin said, smiling at her.

"I am so sorry to ask this but do you mind if I get a quick picture? I would just be so mad at myself if I walked off and didn't do that."

"Sure, of course," Justin said.

She took out her phone and held it in front of them, taking a photograph. Justin was used to these and he had a smile he did for all of them. I watched him lean in and perform this smile like the pro he was.

Mrs. Martin thanked him and walked ahead of us toward the game.

"I told you," I said once she was far enough away that she couldn't hear me. "And that's not even the students. I'm really sorry, and I'll try to put us sitting to the side, but you might have to take about twenty more selfies tonight."

"Hey, guess what, Katie?" he said, sounding like he was in a good mood.

"What?"

"I don't care. I'm here because I want to be here."

"Good," I said with a little smile.

"I'm the one who asked you if I could come."

"Okay, good. I'm just protective of you, that's all."

"Thank you, KK, but I'm a big boy. I've taken a few selfies in my life."

I laughed. "I know. I saw that smile come out, and I was like… perfection."

"That's what I think about your smile, too," he said.

"Aww," I said, looking a little doubtful and knowing that was too normal and cheesy for Justin to say seriously.

"I'm serious," he said, seeing my expression. "There's this place where your upper lip hits your teeth in a way that looks a little dangerous. I don't know how to say it. It's something that doesn't happen with other people's smiles, and it's just... it's perfection, like you said. So, I wasn't just trying to give you the same compliment you gave me. I already knew your smile was perfect."

Just then, we heard footsteps behind us and we turned in time to see Henry Young bounding toward us, me, he was coming straight for me. He smiled and rushed up to me like he was trying to scare me.

"Oh, my goodness, Henry, I thought you were a madman coming up behind me," I said, smiling at him as he came to walk next to me.

"Are you watching the girls?" I asked.

"Yes, and I'm sorry, but Travis Corson showed me some picture he found on the internet of you with Justin, so I knew you were friends, but dang dude, I never thought I'd see you at a girls' softball game! Old Riverbend, bro! Kicking it with Miss Klein."

"Yep, old Riverbend," Justin agreed, walking and smiling and being the coolest guy in the whole world.

"What are you even doing here?" Henry asked looking around like he must be missing something.

We were walking along the outfield fence toward the third base side of the field where our dugout was located.

"We came to watch the girls," I said, answering Henry.

He was extremely excited and was walking backwards next to us, kind of hopping in order to keep up. "I wish you could have come tomorrow night so you could see us play," Henry said.

"Henry, Coach is looking for you," I said.

The girls' softball coach was motioning to Henry, and I was glad to have the distraction. Henry hesitated but then reluctantly ran ahead of us to talk to the coach.

Justin and I kept walking. "Are you still good?" I asked.

"Yes, Katie. I'm fine with him wanting to talk to me," Justin said. "What was more concerning about that whole interaction was how he had his arm around you."

"That was for like two seconds," I said, smiling at him.

"Two seconds too long," he said. "Does he hug all of his teachers?"

"Everybody hugs everybody over here," I said. "Watch. About three of these girls are about to come over here and hug me right now.

"Hey, what's up? Are you pumped, or what?" I said, hollering at a few softball players who were in the outfield as we approached. We were near a gate, so I stepped inside so that I could hug the three girls who came up to us. Justin stood next to me.

"You girls don't let us get you in trouble," I said, looking toward the coach, who was still talking to Henry.

"Oh, we're already done with warmups," Emma said. "Goofball had us down here looking for the earring she lost out here."

"I think I did," Sara said, gazing out at the field.

Two other players saw us standing there, and they ran up to us. We were standing in foul territory, out of the way, but we still got spotted. There were suddenly five softball players gathered around us.

"You got your boyfriend with you, Miss Klein?" One of the girls from the second group came up to me for a hug while the other one asked that question, so I was distracted and it took me a second to realize what she had said.

By the time it registered in my mind, Justin had already said, "Yes."

I laughed like he was joking, and one girl faked passing out, forcing another girl to catch her. "You heard that? Casey asked if that was her boyfriend and he said *yes! Shheeeoooohhhh*, hot dang, Miss Klein!"

I glanced at Justin with an apologetic expression. These girls were not shy. There were a few of them on the team who said exactly what was on their minds, and two of them were in this group.

"I saw a picture of you with Justin Teague and a bunch of other people at a table," Casey said.

"Are you really her boyfriend?" Sara asked.

Sara wasn't even a loud one. *What was she doing getting in on this?*

"Yes," Justin said.

But at the same time, I said, "No."

"She's lying," Justin said. "She's shy about it, so you ladies shouldn't go spreading it around everywhere."

"Yeah, no, we're not," I said. "Because if we were, my *brother* would definitely already know."

"Her brother doesn't know about it," Justin said, "But I vote for telling him, too."

This caused more than one softball player to say. "Oooooohhhh," in that way that said everyone knew a challenge had been made. The ooohs were so loud that I looked over my shoulder to see if we were drawing stares, which we were.

"Okay, so, good luck and have fun, ladies," I said in a comically matter-of-fact tone. "My professional acquaintance, Justin, and I will be taking our seats right down here on the third base line. So, have fun out there and play good, okay fam?"

I started backing away as I spoke. They knew I was joking around and being lighthearted, but I was hoping to also casually walk away without saying any more about the boyfriend/girlfriend thing.

"It's true!" Justin called. "This is my girl right here, even if she won't admit it yet."

He put his arm around me, smiling and walking with me. The girls responded by another round of whoops. I looked at him, shaking my head and smiling as we walked away.

"Oh, you really did it now," I said to him.

"Good, I meant to do it," he said.

He leaned in and kissed my cheek as we walked, and since they were still staring at us, they again whooped, which made me turn back to them with a silly wide-eyed expression.

There weren't a whole lot of people at that game, thank goodness. Justin and I managed to find a secluded spot that was still close to the bleachers and dugout. I sat next to him and we talked to each other like normal, but I could see people out of my periphery, and they were checking us out.

Two people came over to us within the first inning. They acted like they needed to ask me a question and then they introduced themselves to Justin like they didn't want to be rude. It was cute.

"Can we please hold hands?" he said to me, out of nowhere, in the third inning. Our chairs were right next to each other, but we would have to make the effort to touch, and we hadn't done that. I kept my arm off of the rest intentionally because I knew people were gawking. I stared at him. Both of us had on sunglasses. I couldn't see his eyes, but we were staring at each other, and I smiled.

"We can, but I'm trying to explain that it's better not to unless we're really serious."

"I am really serious," he said. "I've been telling you I'm serious since you came back from Canada. I'm the one giving you time here. The ball's been in your court."

I stared at him with a serious expression for several long seconds. "I didn't even know I had a court," I said.

"Whelp, you do," he replied in a joking, all-business tone.

"If we hold hands right now, Justin, I'm going to have a conversation with my brother."

"And what exactly are you going to tell your brother?" he asked, adjusting in his chair and looking at me with a curious smile.

"That I… like you," I said.

My voice came out as hesitant and vulnerable as I felt, and Justin reached over and grabbed my hand.

Chapter 13

"You're going to tell your brother you *like me*?" he asked. "That's my big punishment for holding your hand?"

Justin readjusted to take a hold of me. He pulled my arm over to him, shamelessly holding onto my hand with both of his.

I tried to look like I was paying attention to the game. We were down six to nothing already, so there wasn't much cheering going on from our section. The innings seemed to be lopsided with our batters going three-up, three-down, and their at bats taking twenty minutes. There had already been a couple of trips to the mound so the coach could talk to our pitcher, and it was only the third inning. Our coach had just called another time out.

"Tell Mac," Justin said. "I want him to know you like me. I'm not scared of that."

I took a second to think about it and then smiled at him. "Maybe you should be," I said.

Justin held onto my hand even tighter. "I'm not," he said, confidently.

I grinned at him. I was acting easygoing about everything, but he was melting me. His face, his body, his clothes, and the way he held himself—his smile and his white teeth… and then he went and said things like that. Being next to Justin made me feel like I was swimming in an ocean of warm, magical water—like I was being swept away by something other-worldly. His big hand was wrapped around mine, and I might as well have been in paradise.

We got the third out, and in the bottom of the inning, our bats came alive, and we scored three runs. We held them during the next inning, and then we scored two more, making it a one-run ball game.

I was and had always been a passionate spectator. I came from a family of athletes and we were all cheerleaders because of it. I never yelled insults at an opponent, but I predictably yelled, clapped, and cheered for my team.

During the game, I let go of Justin's hand each time I would want to cheer, and held it again afterward. But then as the game drew to an end, I was unable to sit still. I got to the edge of my seat and would often stand up to cheer or cup my hands around my mouth like a megaphone to yell. Because of this, I was unable to hold his hand during the last inning.

It was tied, and we had to score to win. There were two outs with runners on second and third. The coach called for a bunt, hoping to use that to bring our best hitter to the plate. But we unexpectedly scored on that bunt because of an overthrow.

The girls celebrated and so did we. I yelled and smiled as I watched them collide on the infield.

"You ready?" I said, smiling at Justin once I stopped celebrating.

"Yes." He smiled and leaned in to kiss me on the cheek.

We went through the motions of packing up our chairs, and Justin strapped both of them over his shoulder.

I offered him my hand as we started to walk away, and he smiled at me like he was grateful I did that, which was insane.

We went to tell the team goodbye, and they asked for a picture with Justin. I knew this would happen, and I knew that Justin wouldn't mind. He took pictures with what must have been four different groups, and then he came to me, reaching for the chairs again.

I handed him one of them, but he grabbed the other as well. "It was nice meeting you all," he said, with a wave toward the team since they were all still looking at us. "Great game."

"Yes, amazing game," I said. "That was fun to watch. Good job. I was supposed to go check on Ms. Barbara at the ticket booth, and I couldn't make myself get out of my chair."

Everyone laughed, and I smiled and waved, and used that compliment as our parting words.

Justin got into the driver's seat of my car, and I took out my purse and looked at my phone once we got settled. I had three missed calls and a text from my brother.

"My brother's trying to get in touch with you," I said, reading the text.

"Me?"

"Yeah. He's texting me, asking if you have your phone."

"No, I didn't. I left it in your car, I knew you'd have yours."

"He called three times," I said. "And I think he's looking for you. I wonder what's up." As I said it, I pressed the buttons to call back my brother.

"Hello," he said on the first ring.

"Where are you guys? Where's Justin? I was trying to talk to him."

"He's right here. We're just leaving the game. Justin left his phone in my car. What's up?"

"Can you put him on?" Mac asked.

I handed the phone to Justin. "He wants to talk to you," I said, with a shrug at his curious expression.

"Hello?" Justin said, holding the phone to his ear as he drove. I listened to the one-sided conversation.

"Yeah… no.

(a pause)

Probably about twenty minutes or so…

(pause)

Okay.

Yeah. Okay, see you in a few. Bye."

Justin was smiling when he hung up the phone and handed it to me.

"What'd he say?"

"He was wondering when we'd be home," Justin said.

"Why couldn't he just ask me that?" I asked.

Justin smiled. "He asked us to pick up something on the way home."

"What?"

"Why are you being so nosy?" he asked, smiling.

"Why are you being so secretive?"

"Mac was the one being secretive, actually. I think they just want to buy us dessert or something—probably for watching Victoria.

"Dessert?"

"Yeah. But I think I already said too much. He just said we should meet them somewhere instead of the house."

"For dessert?" I asked.

"Yes, but don't ask me anymore, because I don't know. You now have as much information as I do."

"Do you know where we're going?" I asked.

"Yes."

"Then you know more than me."

"Barely," he said.

I just smiled. I didn't bother asking anything else about it. I didn't care all that much. I didn't mind going anywhere as long as it was with Justin.

"I wonder if Victoria's going to be there," I said.

"You miss her," Justin said, smiling at me.

"I do," I said. "I'm glad Mac's back, and I'm glad I'm not in charge, but I will miss getting so much time with her. At least we still live in the same house," I added, laughing at myself.

***

"The Sweetest Thing?" I asked a while later when we pulled into a shopping center. It was on the corner of 40th and Bank, only a couple of miles from our house. The Sweetest Thing was a new dessert shop that looked vintage but was super hipster, trendy, and expensive. I had only been once. It was the kind of place where the bonbons were five bucks a piece, and a milkshake would set you back ten.

"Mac said for me to wait out here and send you inside by yourself," Justin said, smiling at me once he parked the car. He knew it was ridiculous, and he shrugged before I could even ask.

"Why would they do that?"

"I honestly have no idea. Mac told me they wanted to get you something for babysitting. He said I should drive you here and tell you to walk inside."

I got out of the car somewhat reluctantly. "And he said specifically for me to go by myself? That's weird. Is it sketchy?"

Justin smiled and gestured casually toward the store. "I doubt it. Look at that place," he said. He smiled. "Besides, I can see all the way to the counter from here, so I think you'll be fine."

I looked inside the dessert shop and nodded. "Okay, I'll be right back." I headed inside. I had no idea what my brother was up to, but I figured it couldn't be bad in a place like this.

I thought of our family from Texas. It wasn't uncommon for one of them to plan a trip to come see us, and it also wasn't uncommon for them to plan elaborate ways to surprise us when they did. I half expected my mother or my little brother, Andrew, to be posing as a fake employee behind the counter when I ordered ice cream.

I realized, when I did step through the door, that I had received no instructions and didn't know what to do once I stepped inside. My plan was to head up to the counter, but an employee walked up to me before I made it there. It was a middle-aged woman, dressed nicely and wearing slacks with a denim apron that had the store logo embroidered on it. She approached me with a smile so big that I couldn't help but smile back at her.

"Are you Katie Klein?" she asked. She came to stand close to me and rested her hand on my shoulder.

I had to pull back a little to focus on her. "I am," I said.

"You've got a surprise waiting for you, right this way." She was smiling, and I was smiling, and I glanced back to see if I could see Justin. The sun had already gone down, but there were lights in the parking lot and I could see my car. I couldn't see inside, but I knew Justin would see me and he knew that I was okay.

I followed the woman down a hallway.

"I have to tell you, this is the most excitement we've had in here all week. All year."

"Where in the world are we going?" I said. I must have had hesitation in my tone because she said. "Oh, it's wonderful. I promise you that. This is one of our private rooms. We use it for birthday parties and tea parties. Someone's here to surprise you. They've already ordered a ton of sweets and treats for you to enjoy."

She stopped in the hallway and smiled at me before positioning me next to the door with my back to the wall. The lady must've been a kindergarten teacher in a former career because she turned me by the shoulders and put me into place like nobody's business.

"One whole minute exactly," she said, staring straight at me. "Count all the way to sixty and then turn this handle and walk into that door." She reached up and gave two loud raps on the door, smiling at me like this was all very routine and something she did all the time.

"Count to sixty starting now, okay?"

I wanted to get out of there. I wanted to tell her that I had a someone waiting in the car. But I stayed quiet. The more I thought about it, the more I figured Justin was in on this. I wondered if he would be on the other side of the door when I opened it. I figured mom and dad had come in from Texas. My heart raced a little as I waited, wiggling slightly as I leaned against the wall.

Then, after a while, I realized I was not counting, so I started at twenty-three, which seemed like a reasonable guess at how much time had passed.

I finished counting to sixty, just like I had been instructed, and then I turned to the door, grabbed the handle and pulled. I fully expected to see my parents standing there, but there was only one person in the room.

"Heath?"

"Hey," he said, looking breathless, pitiful.

"Hey?" I said. I knew my expression reflected my absolute confusion.

"Come in," he said, he stepped forward, and motioned me inside. It was an unbelievably beautiful room, decorated like the Mad Hatter's tea party.

Heath gestured toward the table. There was enough dessert on it for the softball team and their families to come eat. There was a fortune in food set out on this table.

"I didn't know what you wanted, so I ordered one of everything," he said.

There were at least twenty ice cream cones set out and waiting. They were gorgeous and perfect, all set out on these little individual stands in every flavor.

"There was just, like, ten people in here," Heath said, swaying a little and making a face like he experienced a whirlwind. "They left out of that door about two seconds before you came in" He pointed behind himself. "Katie, I need to talk to you," he added, looking at me with a beseeching smile. His face shifted and he changed, looking pitiful. He was an incredible actor. He had a face for it. I was compelled to stare at it—compelled to feel for him.

"I should have come after you that day," he said. "I'm so sorry. I knew you were lying about being sick, and I was just hurt and mad. But then I realized I put you in a tough spot, Katie. I rushed you. I should have made it clear that I didn't expect anything to happen between us that night."

Chapter 14

Justin

Justin saw Katie walk into the dessert shop and talk to a lady for a second before heading around a corner where he could no longer see her. She was smiling as she walked back there, so he figured he could just relax and wait on her. His phone was in the console, and he could have fished it out, but he went for the radio instead.

The station Katie had it set to was playing a classic rock song by Tom Petty. He liked it, but he went to the next station, just in case. It was rock. Heavy guitar rock—something he didn't recognize. He was about to turn it back to Tom Petty when he heard a thud as something hit the car. He instinctually reached out and turned the music off completely.

A quick glance in the side mirror showed that someone was walking up. It was Mac. He was followed by Morgan with Victoria riding on her hip. Mac and Morgan were smiling, but Victoria looked tired. Justin felt like he was too low to the ground in Katie's car, and he got out as soon as he noticed them approaching.

"Thank you so much for getting her here so quickly," Mac said. "We've kind of been waiting on you two. Bri was the one who made the whole plan, so I didn't know about it until the last minute. She's in there already. We're supposed to go in, too." Mac gestured to the dessert shop. "Morgan and I are tired, so we probably won't stay long."

"What plan?" Justin asked smiling and feeling better knowing that Katie was in there with her cousin.

"We're all about to go in there and have all the desserts we can handle, courtesy of my sister's boyfriend."

Justin wondered what desserts he had purchased without knowing it, and then he realized in a short, surreal sequence of thoughts that Mac was talking about someone else. His blood turned hot. Mac was still smiling, but Justin's face fell.

"Who are you talking about?" Justin asked in a voice that sounded like it wasn't his own. The tension of the moment seemed to make time stand still. Justin got a sick feeling in his stomach and he moved forward, taking a step away from Mac and Morgan—toward the building—toward Katie.

"Who's in there?" he asked in an impassive tone. He stared straight at Mac, and Mac's smile fell.

"Heath Vick," Mac said. He tried to smile again, but he abandoned the idea when he saw Justin's face break into a pained grimace.

He threw his arm back pointing at the storefront. "Is she in there with him?"

"Yes," Mac said, not seeing the problem.

"Mac, what are you doing?" Justin's tone was impassive, and he instantly began to take off. He wasn't planning on waiting for Mac or Morgan or even taking time to explain. He just headed toward the store. "She doesn't like that guy!" he yelled from over his shoulder as he walked off.

"Justin!" Mac sprang into action, following Justin, who hesitated reluctantly a few feet from the front door. "We're supposed to give them some time," Mac said. "There's a whole plan. He's got a video of a song he wrote. He showed it to me. He's sitting next to Ed Sheeran, who is playing guitar and singing backup." Mac cracked up and shook his head. "I don't know what went down between him and Katie in Canada. But Ed Sheeran? That's next-level boyfriend stuff."

Mac was amazed, and Justin was about to explode. He physically felt like he would combust if he stood there any longer.

"Where is she?" he said in a slow, grimly serious voice that made Mac's expression change.

He pulled back, regarding Justin, taking in how angry Justin was. He was calculating. "What's wrong with you?" Mac said.

"Katie's mine, Mac." Justin made the statement with no apology or uncertainty whatsoever. He was looking Mac directly in the eyes.

Morgan gasped when she heard him say that, but Mac just stood there. He stared directly at Justin, and for what must have been five full seconds. He just peered into his eyes, searching, thinking. "You better go get her, then," Mac said. He shook his head and looked a little uncertain, but Justin didn't hesitate.

He was relieved that he didn't have to explain anything else to Mac. He went into the store as quickly as he could, weaving through groups of customers as he scanned the rooms, looking for Katie, Bri, or even Heath—anyone.

He heard someone utter his name. A lot of people in Seattle were Seahawks fans, and Justin had a recognizable face, so he got noticed quite a bit when he went out. He didn't stop when he heard his name because he saw the people out of his periphery and he knew it wasn't Katie.

Finally, he laid eyes on the woman who had talked to Katie in the first place.

"Hey, can you tell me where you took Katie Klein?" he asked, coming up to her in a hurry.

"Oh, yes, sure. Of course, I'd be happy to take you over there. Just follow me."

She turned and started walking through the shop, but she was walking slowly and it looked like they were going a different direction than she had taken Katie.

"Didn't Katie go that other way?"

"Oh yeah, but we have to reach her from over here."

"What does that mean, reach her?" Justin asked, clinching his fists as he walked.

"Oh, I just mean there's two doors that lead to that room. And this way is actually shorter, anyway."

She was moving way too slow, but Justin had no choice but to follow her.

"Listen, whatever you guys don't eat, we'll pack up and send home with you. Choose what you want once you get in there, and we'll put your things into a box."

She looked back and grinned at Justin.

"It's such a pleasure to have you in the store, Mister Teague. We're all big fans over here. I don't know what to do with all the famous people coming in tonight."

"Thank you so much. Is this where Katie..."

But Justin cut off in mid-sentence because he saw Bri and Ozzy standing there, on the far side of a giant kitchen, twenty feet away.

"Where's Katie?" Justin said, not caring that he was speaking loudly or that there were other people in the room.

"Oh, she's, in our Mad Hatter room, but we still have three more minutes before we can go in. We've been given strict instructions not to open that door until..." The woman pointed at a digital wall clock as she walked.

Justin looked at her like she was crazy if she thought he was about to wait another three minutes.

She smiled at his confused expression.

"We were given strict orders to give them six minutes together. I think Mister Vick has a video he wants to show her."

But the lady's voice sounded distant and muffled because Justin's thoughts were not with her. All he could think about was getting to Katie. By this time, they were nearing the door. Bri and Ozzy were there, along with Charlotte, one of Ozzy's friends from school. The three of them were standing near the door, and Justin went to it.

"Is Katie in here?" he asked, looking straight at Ozzy.

Ozzy nodded.

"Yes," the lady said. "But we have to wait for her and Mister Vick to finish with their—oh, heavens!" She gasped and called out when Justin reached out and turned the handle. It was locked, and Justin shook it hard. "Oh, for goodness sake," she said. "I'm sorry, it won't open like that. I have to scan my card."

By this time, Mac and Morgan were being ushered into the kitchen by a different employee. Justin could see them, but he didn't stop to talk. He kept his hand on the handle and stared at the lady like he was waiting for her to unlock the door. She had a lanyard on and she nervously stepped forward to scan a small box by the door.

Justin turned the handle again, and this time it opened.

"Sorry, we're early!" the woman yelled behind his back, announcing their arrival as he stepped inside.

He could hear Mac and his family talking behind his back, but Justin could think of nothing besides getting to Katie. She was on the other side of the big, elaborately decorated table. Heath was over there, too, and Justin took the route that would put him closer to Katie.

She smiled when she saw him and headed his way. "I was just talking to Heath," she said. "Telling him you guys were waiting for me outside—that you'd be in here any second."

She came to Justin, looking straight at him, caring most about him.

"Are you okay?" he asked.

"Yes." she lowered her voice as she came near him.

Bri, Ozzy, Mac, Morgan and Victoria all came into the room behind Justin, but Katie kept her eyes trained on Justin. She spoke so softly that he was the only one who could hear her.

"This is so awkward," she said. She spoke stiffly as she stared straight at Justin. "There was a whole song. I feel like I'm in a movie right now."

"What kind of movie?" he asked, not speaking as quietly as she was."

"What do you mean?" she asked.

"Is it the kind where I come in here and cause a scene?" he asked.

"I don't think so." She spoke stiffly with wide eyes, and Justin could see how shaken she was. It was rare that her mouth was in an actual straight line. Usually, there was an underlying smile to her appearance. He felt like he could see the pulse in her neck. She was nervous and shaken, and he reached for her instinctually.

She took a hold of Justin's forearm, standing near the table and staring at any spot. She focused blankly on some pie and ice cream as she spoke. Her voice was loud enough to address the whole room.

"I'm—" She cut off when her voice cracked and she cleared her throat. "I'm sorry, but I think there's been a misunderstanding. I see that there's been a lot of planning and I really thank you for going to all this trouble, but I was already here with Justin before I knew any of this was happening. The timing is terrible, and I'm embarrassed, and I really don't know what to say or where to go from here, but my heart is… my heart is… (She hesitated for way too long.) already… sort of… Justin's."

Another gasp came from Morgan, and a whimper from Bri, but it was otherwise quiet.

Heath made a noise of disgust and turned and stalked out of the other direction without a word to any of them.

"Mister Vick!" the lady said.

Heath didn't pay any attention to her. He just walked out, closing the door behind him. She followed him, scurrying past everyone else. "Excuse me, excuse me, I'll make sure he gets out okay."

And she, too, was gone just like that.

Katie focused on Justin again. They found themselves in good company, and there was nothing he could do to resist her. He reached for her and she reached back, holding onto his arm.

She latched onto him so tightly that Justin just went ahead and pulled her into his arms.

"Obviously, we didn't know that guy was going to be here or we would have told you guys something before—"

Justin began to speak, but Katie cut in nervously, smiling at Mac as she started to talk. "Yeah, we were planning on telling you guys something about this tonight."

"The ice cream is melting," Victoria said.

Justin and Katie both looked at her, and Ozzy snapped a wide angle shot of the whole stunned group.

Chapter 15

Katie

My world had just been flipped on its end, but I had Justin there, so everything was okay.

It had been the oddest ten minutes in all of eternity. Justin and I were connected by holding hands, and it was the only thing that kept me from feeling like I was going to spin out of control.

"What just happened?" Bri said.

"The ice cream is melting," Victoria said again.

Morgan walked around to the other side of the decorated table to let Victoria chose an ice cream cone.

"Sorry about the pictures," Ozzy said, snapping away. "This room is amazing, and honestly your expressions are all pretty priceless right now. I'm not going to publish any of these without you looking at them."

Justin pulled me closer, and I went to him, holding onto him and feeling like there was no place I would rather be. Classical music was playing in the background. I hadn't noticed it until now.

"What is this all about?" Bri said, gawking at us and speaking in an animated tone.

"Yeah, what is this?" Mac asked, shaking his head. "Seriously, JT, you've got to tell me if you're checking out my sister."

Justin pulled back to stare at me. "I'm checking out your sister," Justin said seriously to my brother while staring at me. I smiled, not taking my eyes off him. (*Snap, snap, snap,* went Ozzy, and I didn't mind.)

"Oh, my gosh, I can't believe what I'm seeing," Morgan said.

Bri made a noise of agreement. "Yeah, me neither. I knew Heath was coming, and I encouraged him to." I glanced at her, and she regarded me with an apologetic expression. "I had no idea. I am so sorry. I would never have put you on the spot like this."

"I'm sorry, but is anyone else not knowing what to think about this?" Mac gestured to Justin and me. We were still latched onto each other, and we didn't back away when Mac said that and everyone looked at us. "Are we thinking this would be a good idea? Or is it just something you're doing to get Heath to go away?"

"Mac!" Morgan said.

"What? I'm serious."

"They really like each other," Morgan said.

"And I think I saw it coming. I noticed a few things over the last few months, really."

She set Victoria down and then handed her an ice cream cone before choosing one for herself. The two of them went to find seats at the Mad Hatter's table. Charlotte went over to them, and Ozzy put down his camera and went over there as well, leaving my brother there, staring at us.

"We'll talk to you later about it," Justin said to Mac. "But just know that everything's okay and I love her." He spoke quietly enough that the others at the other side of the table assumed they were being left out of the conversation and went on talking to each other. "We're going to take some dessert and go home, but we can talk about it there."

"Yeah," I agreed, nodding at Mac and knowing how awkward this must have been for Justin. "You guys eat whatever you want and then take some home. If there's leftovers, I'll have them package the rest of it and send it to the coaches at my work. It won't go to waste over there." I reached out to touch my brother. I took his hand and gave it a squeeze. "Thank you for rolling with this," I said. "This is still new, and we didn't mean for it to come out before we had the chance to tell you."

"How long has it been happening?" Mac said.

"Not long," I said. I smiled at him because I could tell, just from his demeanor that he was fine with it. "We'll talk to you about it at home," I added.

I grabbed an ice cream cone for myself and a second one for Justin.

"Justin's going to take me home since I have work in the morning," I announced to everyone. "I might see you at the house, but we're heading out. I told Mac for y'all to take what you want, and tell them to send the rest to Riverbend. If the lady has any questions, she can just... call me."

"Don't worry about it," Bri said. "I'll take care of it all this. We'll take some, and I'll tell her to send the rest to your work."

"Thank you," I said. "The athletic department, please." I made an awkward face. "Unless, you know, he wants it, or whatever." I shrugged and held up my ice cream to her, and she did the same to me with hers.

"The ice cream is going to melt," Bri warned. "I'm not going to be able to salvage any of that."

"I know, I figured they'd go to waste. That's why I picked two of them." I waved with the cone in my hand. "Thank you for dealing with this. Love you! See you at home."

I tried to make it seem as casual as possible. I felt bad for Justin that he had to interact with Heath, and I wanted to make the exit go easy for him. I held our ice cream and led the way out of the store and back to my car. I walked quickly and he followed me, holding doors since my hands were full.

Neither of us knew where Heath had gone, but we didn't waste any time getting to the car. Thankfully, there was no sight of him. I handed Justin a cone once he sat in the driver's seat, and we both went to work licking since the ice cream was getting softer.

I had napkins in my glove compartment, and I retrieved some of them to wrap around our cones. There was a little piece of paper wrapped around the cone, but we needed reinforcements. I wrapped a napkin or two around mine before handing the rest of them to Justin.

"Thank you," he said. "Poor little Victoria was probably like, *what happened just now.*"

"She's content with the ice cream," I assured him.

Justin started the car and glanced over the console, smiling at me with a rueful grin. "Dang," he said.

"What dang?"

"I was expecting your parents or Andrew."

"Me too," I agreed, shaking my head dazedly, taking another lick of my ice cream cone. "What a waste of all that ice cream."

Justin let out a little laugh.

"What?"

"It's funny that you think that was the only thing wrong with that situation."

"You're right, I'm sorry," I said. "I should ask you if you're okay. I'm sorry you had to see him."

"I'm fine," he said. "It's just a bummer about that ice cream shop. That used to be one of my favorite places."

He pulled out of the parking spot at the moment he made that statement, which made it seem like he was never planning on going back there.

"It's *still* one of my favorite places," I said. "I'm really sorry for you, because I'd be so ticked off if Gretchen had some big display set up for you. But from my perspective, I just had two dudes fighting over me, followed by me ending up with the only one I ever wanted, followed by that same guy also telling my brother that he loved me. Then I got ice cream—chocolate ice cream in a Davis cone, my ultimate favorite combination. So, I hate it for you, and I'm sooo sorry he was there, I really am, but nothing was ruined for me." I reached over and put my free hand on his arm. "In fact, seeing him only made me realize how much I..."

He turned to glance at me when I trailed off, taking a lick of my ice cream cone. "How much you what?" he asked.

"I was going to say how much I wanted you, but it sounded cheesy."

"No, it doesn't," he said, driving.

"Well, then I'll say it because it's the truth. Seeing you next to him made me want to do anything to make sure I end up with you. Having you both next to each other... it was like one of you was clearly the right one and the other wasn't even close. At no moment during the interaction did I consider whether or not I would rather be with him. It was always you. You were the only one in my mind the whole time. I honestly don't even know why he did that. But I'm happy, and I barely even consider that a hiccup in our evening."

We stopped at a traffic light, and Justin turned to me. "What do you have there?" he asked, looking at my cone.

"Just plain chocolate," I said.

"Yeah, but you called it something else. You said something about the cone.

"Oh, it's a Davis cone. See how it's got the sprinkles? That's what that's called."

"What's mine called? Just plain?"

"It's a plain waffle cone. Mine is a Davis cake cone. You can get a Davis cake or Davis waffle."

"What, do you work in an ice cream shop or something?" he asked, teasing me.

I laughed, feeling relieved that he was in a good mood. "I could probably work in one," I said. "I really like ice cream. There's an ice cream shop on the Strand back home and I love going in there. I've asked for a Davis cone ever since I was a little girl."

We made our way down Bank Street.

"I don't know how you do it," he said. "When I turned that handle and you were locked in that room, I was ready to fight. I was ready to go in there and take no prisoners. And then you act all calm and say a few words, and he leaves, and everything goes back to normal. Now I'm all calmed down, talking about waffle cones."

I laughed. "You don't look like you're all calmed down," I said. Justin was sitting forward in the seat, leaning toward the steering wheel.

"I'm not. I'm not mad, but I'm still amped up. I need to go to the gym and get my adrenaline out."

We were on Bank Street and there was no traffic. I told Justin to pull over. I told him my mom used to make Mac run home next to the car when he needed to get some energy out. Justin liked my idea, and went with it instantly. He still had ice cream left, but he handed it to me, and I balanced both of them in one hand while I drove slowly the remainder of the way home. Justin ran alongside me as I passed two other houses and then pulled into our driveway.

I stopped to let him go in front of me once we got to the driveway and I pulled in behind him. I didn't mean to put myself in a position where I was driving behind him, shining a light on his backside, but there I was, and I figured there was nothing wrong with admitting that the view was glorious.

Even in jeans, Justin moved smoothly and easily for how fast he was running. He stopped in the driveway near the spot where he knew I would park. He was smiling at me and catching his breath when I got out of the car. I got out and went straight to him.

Justin reached out for me, pulling me into his arms and rubbing his face against me. He was still catching his breath, and his chest rose and fell. He was breathless and full of raw masculine energy and there was nothing I could do to hold onto those cones. I just let them fall out of my hand carelessly so that I could take a hold of his face.

I touched him lightly so that he could continue to catch his breath. My fingertips touched his cheek and hairline and I stared directly into his eyes.

"I didn't care about them, either," he said with a little smile. He was still regulating his breathing, but it was steady now. Feeling and seeing him breathe next to me made me see him for the football player he was. I was so close to him and comfortable next to him that I had almost forgotten that he was a first-string NFL running back. But I saw him as a hot-shot athlete in that moment. I felt his body moving next to me, and I marveled at the masculinity.

"I need you," I said, feeling unbelievably vulnerable at that moment. I was in love with him. I could feel it in my bones.

He stared at me like he was the one who was smitten. "Good," he said. "I want you to need me." He was about to kiss me when we saw headlights pull into the driveway.

Chapter 16

Ozzy and Charlotte pulled into the driveway right after Justin and I got home. We all had our normal parking spots, and Ozzy, rather than pulling to the right and parking in his, stopped with his lights shining brightly onto us. He left his SUV running and got out.

Justin and I didn't move. We just stayed there, standing loosely in each other's arms, not looking at Ozzy. We knew it was him, but we didn't look that way since we would've been blinded by the light. We just stared at each other as if wondering why he would stop in the middle of the driveway.

"Who put that ice cream like that?" he yelled.

I turned to look at the way the ice cream fell near my feet.

"No, no, no, don't move!" Ozzy called urgently. "Actually, do move, but not yet, not yet, not yet. Wait till I get over there. I'm going to tell you where to stand. Stay exactly where you are for now." He looked into the vehicle. "Come on Charlotte. I need your help."

Ozzy was an art school dude. He was thinner than Mac and Justin simply because he didn't spend his life working out and being physical for a job like they did. He was still an athletic guy, but he looked and dressed differently than them. He was wearing black jeans and vintage looking lace-up boots. I was able to focus on him and Charlotte as they approached us.

"Go adjust her hair," Ozzy said. "Make it to where it's not laying funny in the back like that."

"Thanks," I said sarcastically.

I stayed still and Charlotte came over to do something to my hair.

"Wait, before you do that. Katie and Justin, you guys stay just like you are but take two steps back and that way." Ozzy pointed directly where he wanted us to stand, and we went there. He stooped down and aimed his camera at us. "Okay three inches that way and then hold it. Charlotte, fix her hair and then please do something with the way her shirt is flopped over in the front."

"Wow, thanks, Ozzy," I said, pretending to take it personal and causing Justin to smile at me.

Ozzy owned several cameras and he had the small one in his hand as he got down, all the way on the concrete, close to the discarded ice cream cones. He stared at the mess seriously before leaning in to adjust the cones the slightest of centimeters this way and that.

"These landed so perfect. This is a really cool shot," he said. "But we're going to lose it if we don't do this now." He quickly shifted, getting onto his side and staring at the camera, lining up the shot. "Okay, you two are in the background of this. An afterthought, really, a blur in the distance. But listen, that's why I need you to pop. Justin, hold onto her.

Put your right hand around her back and your left on her face like you're about to kiss her.

"No problem," Justin said, instantly doing as Ozzy instructed.

"Pull her closer," Ozzy said, clicking photographs the whole time.

He moved around the cones, getting slightly different perspectives on the same frame.

"Okay, we're melting over here. Do whatever you want to do for these last few shots. Good. Yes. The foot. Good. Get comfortable. Great. Okay, now you can kiss if you want to."

Justin grinned at me just before he kissed me.

His lips. I didn't even care that it was happening in front of my cousin and his friend. I was so entranced by Justin's kiss that we might as well have been completely alone. He kissed me lightly even though I would have let him not be so gentle. He held onto me by the waist, pulling me to him and doing it several times.

"Okay, I got the shot, geez! You guys get a room."

"You're the one who told us to kiss," I said, pulling away from Justin with a little smile aimed at Ozzy. I went to the ice cream. "Are you done with these?" I asked Ozzy, pointing at the cones.

"Yes, and thank you," he said. "I'll let you know how those pictures came out, but I can tell you right now, they'll be good. That room was cool, but the way these cones fell is perfect. And thank you," he said to Charlotte who smiled and nodded at him. "You got that?" he asked me, referring to the spilled ice cream.

"Yes," I said.

"I'll help you get it," Justin said, coming to stand next to me.

Ozzy went to move his vehicle, so we were no longer in the bright lights.

"Okay," I agreed. "Thank you. I want to go in and take a shower. I have to get up early for a long day tomorrow. It's senior night for the boys."

We began to clean up the ice cream, doing our best to wipe the excess with our napkins. We both had our hands full, so we headed straight inside.

"I know you mentioned hanging out with a couple of guys from the team tomorrow, but I wanted to let you know you're welcome to come with me to the boys' game if you—"

"Yes," Justin said, cutting me off.

"Yes, what?" I asked. I smiled at him as we walked toward the house.

"Yes, I'll go to the game with you," he said. "Isn't that what you were asking me to do?"

"Yes, yes, definitely."

He stopped and opened the door, and I walked inside and closed the door behind us. We walked to the trashcan and then both of us went to the sink to wash the stickiness off of our hands. Justin was going to let me go first, but I made room for him in such a way that he knew I wanted him to come stand beside me.

"I just assumed you weren't coming with me because you mentioned going to Mike's."

"We're all getting together at Mike's at three o'clock," he said. "I'll still be able to spend a few hours with them and then meet you at Riverbend afterward. If you want me to," he added.

I looked at him, wondering how in the world my life had come to Justin wanting to tag along with me. I was used to hanging out with him on a regular basis, but there was never a time in our friendship where I felt like he liked me.

Right now, however, he was looking at me like he would follow me anywhere.

"Of course I want you to," I said.

I was a little nervous, but I reached out for his arm, which was lined with hard muscles. Due to the nature of his position, his forearms had taken a lot of hits. They were muscular from this, and my body had physical reactions from touching him there. His skin was soft, but his arms were hard and substantial, and I tugged him to me.

We stood in the kitchen, and I leaned against a counter, pulling him in. Justin came to me without hesitation. He stepped right in front of me, letting his body lean against mine. He wasn't huge for a football player, but he was big compared to me, and I stared up at him, feeling breathless.

I didn't know what to say. If I had a metaphor for our relationship, it would be a slide. I felt like we had been climbing up the steps for almost a year, and now we had reached the top and we were about to let go and let ourselves enjoy the ride.

"What are you thinking?" he asked, seeing me stare blankly at him.

"I'm happy you're coming with me," I said. "I didn't know you could be done at Mike's in time. Last time you went over there, you stayed all evening. You guys went fishing and everything."

"We did, and we'll fish tomorrow. He lives right on the water. I'll just leave when I'm ready."

"Well, it starts at six-thirty, but it's senior night and they have a little presentation beforehand. They probably won't get started until seven. And, you know, they play nine innings, so it's longer. You don't need to be there right on time."

He came close to me, ducking and putting his face near my neck and ear. I stayed still, my heart racing. Justin invaded my space so tenderly and so intentionally that when he opened his mouth to speak, I fully believed he was going to say something to proclaim his love to me.

"You need to go to bed," he said.

"I do," I agreed, remembering to breathe. My pulse was racing. My arms were positioned between us with my hands resting on his chest.

"You should go," he said. "Mac will be back soon enough, and he'll have a hundred questions for us. Just let me talk to him, and you go get your stuff done for work in the morning."

"Okay," I said, knowing I had a long day coming tomorrow. "I'll text you in a little while. I might see you later tonight, and if not, then definitely tomorrow."

He nodded. "Riverbend at six-thirty."

"Yeah. I'll bring the chairs. They're already in my car. We're playing South Kitsap, so it'll be crowded."

"Is it in the same place we went tonight?" he asked.

"Yeah. Basically. It's the bigger field. You'll find it."

Ozzy and Charlotte came into the room and I instinctually took a step to the side, breaking contact with Justin. It wasn't that I wanted to, it was just that I knew it was a lot for my family to take in, and I hated to go from nothing to constantly touching each other. I knew Justin would understand, and he seemed to.

We were both smiling at Ozzy and Charlotte when they came into the kitchen.

"Thanks for letting me get that shot," Ozzy said. "I've already looked at it and it was really cool. I'll send you guys the result once I get it edited."

"And thanks for the cake," Charlotte said.

"No problem," I said. "I'm glad you got some."

"Bri and Morgan were talking about packing a bunch of it up to bring home." she said.

150

"Cool, cool," I said, feeling like every moment that I wasn't holding onto Justin was awkward.

I was exhausted. I had been up since six, and I had to do it again tomorrow. Not only that, but it had been a day full of unusual, thought-consuming events. I wanted to take Justin up on his offer to handle things from here. I was thankful that he said that. I took a deep breath and smiled at the three of them.

"Okay, goodnight, you guys. I'm going to bed."

Chapter 17

Justin

He could not stop thinking about Katie.

She went to bed early, and he stayed up, talking with Mac about her and telling Mac the truth from his own perspective.

Katie went to work the following morning, and Justin thought of her so continually that he did the only thing he could think of that might help him—he bought her something.

He went to the jewelry store and bought her a sixteen-inch gold chain. He wanted to buy her a ring, but he knew he shouldn't rush it, so he bought a necklace instead. It was perfect for her. The woman in the store tried it on for him, and he was clearly able to imagine Katie wearing it. He could see right where it would fall on Katie's collarbone, and he knew he had to buy it for her.

The lady boxed it and wrapped it, and Justin took it with him to the game. He had on some cargo shorts, a t-shirt, and ball cap from when he was over at Mike's, and he stuck the necklace box into his pocket.

He talked with one of the parents as soon as he walked toward the field. She recognized that he had been with Katie the night before and she came right up to him to let him know where he could find her. It was only six o'clock, so he wasn't surprised Katie wasn't out there.

Justin wasn't even planning on looking for her. He got there earlier than he thought he would, and his plan had been to find a quiet spot to sit and wait for her—maybe answer a few texts.

But the lady ushered him across two fields before stopping and pointing. "It's that building right there where the baseball team is coming out. Miss Klein is in there."

"Okay, thank you," Justin said.

He talked to Henry Young when he walked past the team. "Miss Klein's in there talking to Ty and Brice and all them," Henry said. "All those big linebacker boys know there's free food on senior night." Several team members laughed at his joke.

Justin thanked them, wished them a good game, and kept on walking toward the building. He walked into an empty entryway, but he heard talking and saw lights from a room on the left.

He heard Katie's voice as he came up. "No, no, no, no, y'all stop. I'm not trying to burn him. It's not like that. It's not personal. I'm trying to help him, and I'm doing it in front of all of you because he's not the first one I've heard say it. I want you guys to sound smart when you get out of here, and you need to know you don't *go to college* for football. I hear you guys say that all the time. You go to college for history, or biology, or art, or business."

"I'm going for communications," one of them said.

"I'm going for women," another one said, laughing and causing others to laugh.

"All right, but just so you know, you go to college for a subject, and you play football while you're there. I've heard most of you say it, so don't laugh at Brice or say I'm trying to burn him. I believe in you enough that I want you to look and sound smart."

"Aww, you know we love you, Miss Klein."

"Yeah, we do but you don't have to teach us all that stuff. You can just introduce us to your brother."

"Or to her boyfriend," someone else said. "I heard she had Justin Teague at the girls' softball game last night."

"Yeah, just introduce us to your boyfriend," another one said.

"He can't get you a spot on the team," I said. "You guys have another thing coming if you think he can do that. You're the only one who can do that."

"Well how am I supposed to do it if I can't even get my teacher's brother to put in a good word for me?"

"He would, but good words only go so far, Brice I'll definitely give you a good word once you get to be the best... what position do you play? Offensive tackle, right?"

"Yes ma'am, right guard," he said.

"What do you do?" She asked. "You're supposed to keep the quarterback safe? Is that right?"

"Yeah," he said.

"Then that's what you do, Brice. Become the best in the whole world at that. I've been around multiple professional athletes in my life, and one thing that they have in common is that they all work extremely hard at making themselves the best. You becoming obsessed with training your body to keep a quarterback safe is the only way for you to get what you want. Make yourself a scholar about it— learn how the other great right guards went about keeping their quarterbacks safe. Study them. Ask questions of your coaches and actually think about what they say. Train and condition your body to be a quarterback-keeping-safe machine, you understand? Think about it with your spare time and come up with new ways to do it. You give your thoughts to that and that alone. If you can become the best at keeping a quarterback safe, everything else will fall into place. Colleges, scholarships, coaches, scouts, NFL contracts, cars, money, women—all that stuff is great. I can see why you would want that stuff. But those are not the actual goal they are the by-products of the goal. You have one goal, and thaaat iiis... what, Brice?"

"Keeping a quarterback safe," he repeated sounding reluctant and smiling, which made Justin smile also.

"So, go out there and become the best at doing that. And then call me, and I'll get my brother and my boyfriend to get you on their team."

"Yes ma'am," he said, sounding excited.

The other boys started talking and laughing.

"All right, well I have to get out there for the game. Are you guys coming to watch after you eat?" Multiple people answered, some agreeing and others saying they were leaving."

"All right, well, I'll see some of you out there, I guess, otherwise have a good night."

"You too, Miss Klein!"

"Wait, are you coming to my track meet this weekend?" one of them said.

"No, I hadn't planned on going," she said. "But I might. I'll think about going by there. A couple of girls were asking me about it, too."

"Who?"

"Kesha and Allison," she said. "I might go by there. I have to see what's going on. One of you text me the schedule tomorrow morning, if you think about it."

"I will," he said.

Justin could tell that Katie had been coming closer to the door as she spoke, and he stood back and hugged the wall in the hallway, letting her walk past him before he got her attention. He gave her a second to walk toward the door before saying her name gently, trying not to startle her.

"Katie," he said.

She turned, looking a little confused. But she smiled the instant she saw Justin. "Hey," she said, speaking quietly since the doorway to the banquet room was open. "What are you doing here so early? I was just going out to put our chairs up."

She went to him, smiling as she popped up onto her toes, offering her cheek for a kiss. Justin was happy to do it. He placed his lips on her cheek for a quick kiss before both of them walked lightly out of the building.

"I wanted to come early so I could give you something," he said.

"What is it?" she asked, looking at his hands like she half-expected him to be holding something.

They walked outside, behind the practice field headed toward the boys' field, which was already bustling with action.

"Do you want it now?" he asked.

She beamed at him. "Yes. Where is it?"

"In my pocket."

"It's not a ring, is it?" she asked.

She was so casual about it that Justin said. "No, why? Would you have said 'yes' if it was?"

"Oh, an *engagement* ring?" she asked.

"What other kind of ring would it be?"

"Is that what you got me?" she asked.

"No."

"Is it a red rubber ball?"

"No, and those two things couldn't be more different."

"Which one is it closer to?" she asked. "The ring or the ball?"

"The ring."

"Is it *jewelry*?" she asked in a disbelieving tone.

He smiled. "Yes."

"What'd you get me?"

"Would you have said 'yes' if it was a ring?"

"Well I don't know, Justin. I can't imagine myself saying 'no' to you, so whatever that means." She made eye contact with him. "But it's not a ring, anyway, so we don't have to think about it."

He followed her, and they walked toward the concession stand where she had stored the chairs.

"What do you think it is?" he said.

"A key ring?"

"A *key ring*? Why would I get you a key ring? That's not jewelry."

"It's close to jewelry. And I don't want you getting me anything expensive." She glanced at him and he shrugged.

"Well, it's not expensive to me," he said easily, smiling and shaking his head and making her laugh. He could tell Katie didn't want him to spend money on her. She wasn't used to that. Ever since he knew her, she had wanted to pay her own way. She was stubborn like that. He hoped she would like her necklace and not feel bad about taking it.

They walked alongside each other for several steps before coming to a stop. There was a group of people standing between them and the door, and they stopped before the people could hear their conversation.

"What is it?" she asked.

"A chain. A necklace."

"May I have it?" she asked, blinking at him.

"Sure. Now?"

"Do you have it with you?" she asked.

"Yes."

"I'd love to see it," she said. "No one's ever given me a necklace before."

Justin reached down and retrieved the small rectangular box out of the side pocket of his cargo shorts before handing it to her.

"That's all wrapped up with a bow," she said, staring at the box like she was surprised.

Justin nudged it toward her, and she took it from him a bit reluctantly.

"I didn't know it was going to be in a box."

He let out a little laugh. "Did you think I was going to hand you a loose gold chain?"

"Yes, I sort of did," she said, laughing with him. She glanced at the people who were standing within shouting distance, but they were doing their best to try to give her and Justin privacy.

Katie started to open the wrapper, but Justin put out a hand to stop her so that he could say something. "I couldn't stop thinking about you," he said. "I mean, what kind of girl has movie stars falling all over themselves... and then I see you and hear you with these students, and they're all in love

159

with you, too." He shrugged and hesitated, but then continued with a disappointed sigh, "Honestly, Katie, had I known you would say 'yes', this would have been a ring."

She smiled. "That might be the most romantic thing anyone has ever said to me."

Chapter 18

Katie

"That might be the most romantic thing anyone has ever said to me," I said. And I meant it. I could see that he was serious with the ring comment, and I was touched.

Justin instantly replied, "Let's go to a jewelry store, then. We can trade this in on an engagement ring." I smiled at him, and he said, "I am not even playing."

I was holding the box, and I pulled it away from him in a small motion, causing him to smile at me. "I want to keep what you got me," I said. "We can talk about a ring some other sometime."

"Some other sometime?" he asked, smiling.

I nodded.

I was, in general, much more patient than Justin. He was a grinder by personality. Once he got his mind set on something, there was no stopping him. It was surreal, though, being the thing his affections were fixed on. I could feel that his mind was set on me, and it was wonderful.

I turned my back to the small group of people as I gently but quickly unwrapped the box. My heart was racing as I stashed the wrapping paper in my pocket and then opened the box.

Inside was the prettiest necklace I had ever seen. It was gold and it was the perfect thickness and type of link. I wasn't sure what it was called—it could have been box chain or Cuban link. I didn't care what it was called. I only knew that it was perfect, just my style.

"Oh, my gosh, Justin." I closed the box. "I'm probably going to cry when I put this on. I love it so much." I held the box close to my stomach as I stared into his blue eyes. It's the nicest thing anyone has ever bought me. I've never owned a… jewelry. It honestly makes me feel like a grown up. I feel like only a grown woman would own a chain like this." I pulled back and straightened my shoulders like I had just been given some kind of prestigious award. "Am I a woman now?" I asked, looking surprised and happy.

Justin let out a little laugh and sang, "But she's always a woman to meee," in a Billy Joel impersonation that almost sounded like a pirate.

"That kind of sounded like Mister Crabs," I said, causing us both to laugh. "Hey, let's go get our chairs and set them out, and then you can come with me to my office for a minute so I can get a better look at this and put it on. We'll take the golf cart over there and back so we're not late for senior night."

"Yeah, that's fine," he said, shrugging like he was up for anything.

We went toward the concession stand to get our chairs, and we were, of course, stopped by the group of people who had been standing there the whole time. It was five or six parents and siblings of team members. I had met some of them before, but I knew they were most excited for the chance to talk to Justin. He grabbed my hand as we walked. It was a totally natural motion, and I held onto him easily.

"Looks like rain later," Henry's dad said.

"Yeah, I heard about that. I hope we get the game finished before it rolls in."

"I guess you have Justin Teague with you," one of the women said.

"Yes ma'am. We were just headed back over to the gym for a minute, but we'll be back to watch the game."

They seemed happy to hear that he'd be back and they nodded and smiled and let us pass. Justin and I kept walking past them until we reached the concession stand. We made quick work of setting out our chairs in the back of an area that was already more crowded than the day before.

Then we went to the sidewalk where the golf cart was parked. I drove it quickly, feeling like we were running to something or from something even though we weren't.

I had on a small messenger purse and I had stashed the necklace box in it, but I retrieved it again when we were on the way inside. I asked Justin to wait for me while I went into the faculty restroom. I wanted to let him see me react to the necklace, but I needed a minute alone with it.

It was heavy, and I stared at the way its perfectly polished surface reflected the light. I opened the clasp and put it on my neck. I was wearing a v-neck baseball t-shirt, and it rested on the edge of my collar.

It wasn't a choker, but it definitely wasn't a long necklace, either. I couldn't get enough of it. It was the perfect gift. I never knew that I was missing this chain in my life until I put it on my neck.

I stared in the mirror, blinking away the tears that threatened to fill my eyes. I remembered how he said we could trade it in for a ring, and I smiled at myself in the mirror, thinking I wouldn't trade this thing for the world. I wasn't even a jewelry person, and I officially loved this necklace. I stared at the shiny gold chain, feeling like I never wanted to take it off.

I was happy. It was one of those moments where all was right with the world. I stashed the box in my purse and took ten seconds to freshen up my face and hair before heading back out to the hallway.

"What's in your mouth?" Justin asked me, seeing me bite something as I pushed open the door and made my way to him in the hallway.

"A mint," I said.

"I'll take one of those."

"Oh, shoot. It was the last one, but you can have this one if you want. I just put it in my mouth."

I thought for sure he would deny me, but he said, "I'll take half of it. Just bite it in half."

I smiled at him for a second, but knowing that he was serious, I bit the round candy. Justin saw me do it, and he took me by the waist, leaning in, circling, about to come in for the bite. He rushed me. I barely got the piece of mint ready for him by the time his mouth came to mine.

I was smiling as I leaned up, but I had to stop to get the mint ready for him. I held the larger piece in my teeth and Justin took it from me, his warm mouth coming over mine as he took it in.

I was so anxious to keep him close that I squeezed him. Nobody was in the hallway with us, and I said what was on my mind. "Justin, my necklace!"

"Do you like it?"

"Are you kidding? I love it." I reached up and touched it, letting my fingertips graze the top of my chest where the chain rested. "Thank you for this."

"You're welcome. I wanted to buy you that. It makes me happy to see you wear it."

"That's kind of... I don't know how to put it. It makes me feel happy that you wanted to put a chain on me—even if it wasn't for other people to see, or to prove some protective possessive point."

"Oh, it was to prove that," Justin said easily, smiling at me.

Goodness.

He loved me.

I could feel it.

And I loved him back.

"It looks good on you," he said.

"Thank you. I love it so much, Justin. Seriously." I held onto him as I took off, walking toward the door and onto the sidewalk that would eventually take us back to the golf cart. "I know you said in your text earlier that it went fine, but what did you and Mac talk about last night?"

"Everything," Justin said. "I was honest and told him everything. From my end, at least. He was a little weird about it at first, but we talked about it, and I told him I'm not giving you up, so that's where we ended."

"I haven't heard from him today, but I've been at work all day. Do you think I have anything to clear up with him tonight, or is he all good?" I asked.

"I think he's all good," Justin said. "I'm sure he'll ask you something about it, but I told him we're doing this, and he knows there's nothing he could really say."

We made our way to the golf cart and Justin kissed me once we sat on the seat. His breath still tasted like peppermint, and I remembered him taking half a mint from my teeth. I let out a little squeaking noise at the memory of it. It was so involuntary that I honestly didn't realize I did it until it came out of my mouth. I laughed at myself when I realized what had happened.

"What was that?" he asked.

"Oh, I just squeak sometimes."

Justin grinned at me as I drove. He reached out and held my hand once I got going. He was a gigantic star with the Seahawks. He was just coming off of an incredible season, and everybody in Seattle recognized him and loved him. That was why I wasn't surprised at all when Henry and two other seniors came across the outfield, heading toward us, saying, "Justin! Hey, Justin!"

I stopped on the sidewalk where we could intercept them.

"Mister Teague, Justin, Coach said we could ask if you wouldn't mind… Mister Anderson, Seth's dad was going to throw out the first pitch. He's the Fire Chief. But we were all wondering if you, Justi— Mister Teague, wouldn't mind doing it. You know, if you, if it's not too much to ask."

I was about to tell Henry that maybe we could ask Justin in advance sometime so it's not so spur of the moment. But before I could say anything, Justin spoke.

"I-I would, Henry, but I don't want to take the opportunity away from the Fire Chief."

"Oh, no, no, no, Mister Anderson was the one who…"

"Yeah my dad was the one who asked if you would do it," Seth said. He motioned to a group of men, including his dad and a few coaches, who waved hopefully at us.

Again, I was about to step in on behalf of Justin, but he spoke before I could. "Sure, I'll do it," he said. "If you're sure I'm not stepping on anybody's toes."

"What? Are you kidding? Noooo! No way, dude. Bro. Dude."

The players started shoving at each other out of excitement.

I started to drive off but Henry stopped me. "Wait, Miss Klein. Coach said if number twenty-two agrees, we should keep him over here with us so he can walk out there with us after senior night and everything. He needs to come with us now."

Justin started to get off of the golf cart, and I turned to him.

"You'll be over there for like twenty minutes," I said quietly where only he could hear me.

He smiled. "It's fine."

"You don't have to do any of this," I said. "They already have Mister Anderson. And I don't even know why they're trying to have someone throw out the first pitch at a high school game. You don't have to do it."

Justin cocked his head back, staring at me with that slow, easy confident grin that made me feel all warm and fuzzy. "Yeaaaah, I'm pretty sure they want me to, though," he said. He spoke quietly because the three players were standing there, staring at him, waiting anxiously.

I smiled. "Thank you," I said.

He gave me a shrug. "You don't really owe me anything, but I'll still be collecting some debt for it later tonight."

He got off of the golf cart, smiling at me.

"Okay," I said, casually, speaking where everyone could hear me. "Because I don't like to owe anybody anything."

Justin grinned as he walked, heading for Henry and the others.

"You know where I'll be sitting," I yelled.

"Yeah," he agreed.

I watched Justin meet up with Henry and the boys, and I felt nervous for him. I imagined him being announced and throwing the opening pitch, and I hoped he didn't feel nervous or on the spot. I had seen him do interviews and speak publicly and he did fine. But I had no idea whether or not he could pitch a baseball.

I went to the concession stand and got a drink and some candy for myself and Justin before the game got started.

I got stopped by a couple of people before I made it back to my chair, but they were both conversations that had nothing to do with Justin. I could see Justin with Coach Brown and the others while Senior night took place. They talked to each other, and Justin looked like he was having a fine time.

Everyone at the game cheered like crazy when they announced that the Seattle Seahawks starting running back was going to throw out the first pitch.

It was like a dream. I watched in awe as Justin captivated their attention. He borrowed a glove from Henry, and caught the ball thrown to him by the catcher.

He stood on the mound, and stared past his glove to the catcher. He looked to the side and spit, looking as natural as a pro baseball player. The crowd laughed and cheered when he did that, and Justin smiled just before he reared back, stepped forward, and released the ball.

He took a natural step and had the natural follow through of an actual pitcher. He looked flawless out there—better than our real pitcher. He threw technically, and the ball went directly to the catcher, crossing the plate in a perfect strike.

Dylan Marcantel, the catcher, caught the ball before standing, letting out a whoop and skipping to the side. Out of excitement, he winged the ball back to Justin.

Everyone was pumped about having him there, and they cheered like crazy when he waved and smiled and made a quick, graceful exit through the third base dugout.

Justin found me in no time. He shook a few hands on his way to me, but he reached me quickly. He leaned over me and gave me a kiss before he sat down. Everyone was looking at us, and I did not expect a kiss, but I also did not mind it.

I touched my chain instinctually as he sat next to me.

"That was a good pitch," I said, looking a little surprised.

"What sports did I play in high school?" he asked.

"All of them," I said, knowing that he was a multi-sport athlete. "I knew you played baseball, but I didn't think you'd be a pro pitcher."

He gave me that confident sideways grin. "I'm kind of good at everything."

Chapter 19

Three months later
Late summer

Technically, I had the summer off.

I still went in to keep myself in the loop and get prepared for the fall. But it was nice... I worked a lot less hours and I went in only when I wanted to. It allowed me to share the same schedule with Justin. Both of us were off during early summer, but we continued to work by choice. I got things done while Justin was at the gym, and we matched our schedules so we could still be productive and spend the maximum amount of time together.

We instantly and easily went into couplehood. There was no tiptoeing around my brother or my cousins. In fact, we had already spent time as a couple with my whole family in Texas.

I had a trip planned to Galveston during the first two weeks in June, and Justin came with me and stayed the whole time. To stay in shape, he trained at my uncle Billy's boxing gym. He did strength and conditioning in the mornings, and then some light boxing afterward.

I joined him for that portion a few times, and we had fun boxing together. I had been exposed to fighters since I was a little kid, so I looked like I knew what I was doing even though I was in no shape to keep up with most of the people in that gym. Either way, Justin was impressed, and he made me promise we would put on gloves and mitts when we got back to Seattle.

Everyone in my family had already met Justin prior to that trip. They already loved him, so it was easy for them to accept him as one of us. Every time anyone would mention future plans, they would speak of us as a pair. The trip to Galveston made me feel settled with Justin in a new way. We came back to Seattle with a certain sort of calm, peaceful assurance about our relationship.

That trip was several weeks ago, and in the time since then, we had adopted an easy routine where we saw each other every day. Things would change soon when he and Mac had to go back to training camp and I had to go back to school full-time. But the summer weeks had been wonderful.

Being with Justin was easy.

We were best friends who also loved each other. We also happened to be insanely attracted to each other, but we intentionally held off on that. Both of us had a past. Neither of us were perfect or had made perfect choices, so no one expected us to save ourselves for marriage in this relationship. But we decided to do it, anyway.

We didn't even tell anyone. We made the decision to do that early on in our relationship, and we stuck to it.

Only days ago, I had a conversation about it with my brother. He brought up something that seemed accusatory, and it led me to say point blank that Justin and I were saving ourselves. Mac was so genuinely surprised and excited that I could tell he assumed we had that sort of relationship already.

Little things like that were fun for me. I enjoyed surprising people. The decision itself felt good as well. It wasn't always easy, though. Justin and I had been in situations where we found ourselves alone and had to make the conscious choice to stop. It was difficult at times, but looking back, I felt happy that we were waiting.

Today had been one of those times when I felt nostalgic about our relationship for other reasons. I took care of him after his workout. Justin had a hard day with his leg. He worked out and pushed past it, but his hamstring still felt compromised, and it was something he had battled continually for months and months now. He would continue to work hard and push past it and perform at the highest level, but there were days when he broke down and let his frustration show, and today was one of them.

Earlier, I had massaged his legs with a blend of essential oils that included cypress because it was supposed to help blood flow.

I prayed for him constantly.

That was what I was doing now.

He was sleeping and I was praying.

We were currently at Justin's place, in his living room, sprawled out on his couch in our PJ's. He had fallen asleep about thirty minutes ago and I stayed up to finish the movie we were watching.

His air conditioner was cranked, and we were snuggled on the couch with a thick comforter. He was propped up in the corner, eyes closed, breathing steadily, sleeping soundly.

I had been praying for him, but I forgot. Sometimes I would start thinking about something else mid-prayer and lose concentration.

"And I know it's got to have a point if you're letting him go through it," I said, continuing my prayer in the same extremely quiet voice I had been using since he was sleeping. "I just wish the reason could be over or could be resolved. Maybe the reason is that you want me to pray again right now."

I reached out and put my hand on his leg.

"Please. I know we prayed for it a bunch, I know you have a whole plan, but please, please just do it. I know You can make his leg back to normal. You're better than any doctor. Please, please, please just make it Your will to do it. And I promise we'll give you all the glory. When it gets better tomorrow, I'll tell Justin that I prayed this prayer, and he'll know it worked, and he'll tell all his friends on the team."

I spoke humbly, presenting my plan, but I also pleaded with God like He was my Dad. I spaced out again, thinking about humbleness and making sure my heart was in the right place. I just wanted Justin to be healed so badly. It was a moment later when I continued.

"I know he'll get through it and I do know there's reason for this, but please just help if You want to. Please touch his body. I love You. You're amazing. It's in Jesus's name we pray, amen."

That last sentence was something I said at the very end of almost every prayer, so it came out a little too rushed compared to everything else.

The movie was over and I knew it was time to get Justin to bed so I could go home.

For a second, I contemplated the least jarring way to wake him up, but I quickly went with a light touch on his arm, which was outside the covers.

"Hey," I said.

"Hey," he said.

He answered me so instantly and in such an aware tone that there was no way he had been sleeping. He opened his eyes, smiling at me and pulling me more securely on top of him. There was a layer of comforter between us, and I molded to him comfortably. I pulled back to stare at him. He looked aware and alert.

"Are you awake?"

"Yes," he said, with an amused grin.

"I know you're awake now, but were you awake before I woke you up?"

"Yes."

"For how long? Because it sounded like you were breathin—"

"Marry me," he said, cutting me off in mid-sentence.

"What?"

"That prayer," he said. "The way you pray. I have to have you, Katie. Just marry me."

"That was a… you heard that prayer? That was not even a good… I didn't even know you were awake. I think I trailed off a few times."

I was genuinely a little embarrassed. I remembered myself saying *please, oh, please* to the Lord like I was a little girl.

"Just marry me, Katie," he said. "I can't take it anymore. I need you on my team."

"I am on your team."

"Permanently," he said. "With the ring and the last name and everything."

"Okay," I said after a few seconds. I could tell that he was being serious, and I definitely wasn't going to deny any promise of a future with him.

"Before camp," he said.

"That's next week," I said.

"Is that okay? Does that mean we have to elope? Will you elope with me, Katie?"

"Yes," I said, staring into his eyes.

"Are you scared?" he asked.

"No."

"Do you care where we'll live?" he asked.

"No. I just assumed we'd stay here."

"Are you okay with that?" he asked.

"Yes." I reached up and touched my gold chain with my thumb and pointer finger. I never took it off, and touching it was something I did absentmindedly. "Do you really think we can get it in before camp? Five days. Is that enough time? I've never tried to elope."

"Surely it's enough time," he said. "People make quick marriage decisions all the time, right? I could get the team Chaplain to come help us out if we need it. Can you maybe call the courthouse and see what we need, technically, to get a license?"

Justin was all business when he set his mind to something, and I knew him well enough to know that this conversation was about to lead to me being a married woman by the end of the week.

Katie Teague.

I liked it.

I loved him.

Justin was the man of my dreams, and there was no way I would pass the opportunity to elope with him. He offered and I accepted.

I nodded. "I'll call tomorrow."

He gave me a little squeeze, adjusting me on his lap. "We'll need to tell our families. Mac especially, since we live here."

"I know my brother, and he's going to tell us to stay in the guest house. He's going to say we can just both stay here."

"Can we please just do that plan?" he asked, holding me close like he didn't want me to leave, even for the night.

"Yes."

"When?"

"Soon. This week, hopefully."

"Tonight?" he asked, tugging me stubbornly.

I laughed. "No. Not tonight. Tonight, I have to go back to my room."

Justin let out a disapproving groan and held me tighter.

I laughed and then kissed him.

"I love you," I said.

"I know you do," he said, referring to my prayer. "Thank you for loving me."

I stared straight at him. "It's easy," I said slowly.

"You do it the best," he said.

"Well, I guess that's a good thing because you already asked me to marry you."

"This week," he reminded me. "Before Friday."

"Yeah, before Friday," I agreed.

Justin didn't say he loved me back during that exchange. He didn't have to. I already knew it.

Chapter 20

Four days later

"I cannot believe we did it," I said, shaking and looking at my husband from the passenger's seat later that week.

It was four o'clock on a Friday, and we had just come from the courthouse.

I was officially a married woman.

Pat Cooper, the Seahawks Chaplain, met us up there and performed a ceremony for us. Mac and my cousins came, but Justin didn't have anyone there. It was a brief, simple, sweet ceremony where we both stated that we intended to spend the rest of our lives loving each other.

It was all I needed or wanted, and I was grinning uncontrollably as we drove back to the house. I would spend the night with Justin as my husband. It was something I had thought a lot about, but it hit me again as we were on our way home.

Mac had bought dinner for us all to celebrate, so I knew we had plans to eat in the main house before we went to the guest house. Now that I was officially Justin's wife, I was focused on how quickly we could finish dinner and get home.

It felt natural to me to live wherever he lived. Being next to Justin felt natural. I knew I had made the right choice when I said 'yes'. I was contemplating these things when we pulled up at the house and got out of the truck to go inside.

I wondered if the food was already here or if we would have to wait for it. I realized I had been so preoccupied with making plans to go to the courthouse that I didn't consider the meal afterward or the fact that I would be this anxious to get home with Justin.

I was in a surreal but peaceful, happy, somewhat oblivious state when I walked into the main house and a room full of people all yelled "Surprise!"

There were at least fifty people, all spread out on the far side of the kitchen, a panorama view of all the people I loved most, all staring at me.

Bu-bum, bu-bum, bu-bum, my heart pounded as they yelled and clapped and surprised the ever-living daylights out of me.

Justin drew me in, supporting me physically while at the same time, laughing at my utter shock. Everyone was at the house, and I actually had no idea they were coming. My whole family was there—so many of them—aunts, uncles, cousins, parents, Andrew... I cried as I took in how many people had dropped everything on almost no notice to fly across the country for this. It was overwhelming, and I went from tearing up to full-on boo-hooing within seconds.

I covered my face with my hands and Justin hugged me, shielding me while I got myself together.

"I told you guys she had no idea!" Justin announced, causing everyone to laugh.

"Happy wedding day!" My mom yelled, causing a round of cheers and yells from everyone in the room.

They all came near, gathering around, patting me, hugging me, hugging us, taking pictures, talking, hugging, laughing, dancing, and so on and so forth.

And that was how my surprise, big-deal wedding party happened.

There were close to sixty guests. A few of the immediate family were staying with us at Mac's, but the rest were all staying at the same hotel, here on the island. Even a few from Justin's family had come.

The whole family took a shuttle from the airport to arrive here with no vehicles so that I wouldn't get tipped off. It was a real surprise. They pulled it off without me having a clue.

I was already dazed from getting married, and the party put me way over the top. I spent the evening in a zonked but happy state where I went with anything and I felt like I was the most easy-going person on the planet.

There were so many conversations had, stories told, and pictures taken that I hardly knew which way was up.

It was 9pm before I knew it. The last group was just about to leave for the hotel. We were waiting for the second and final shuttle. Once they left, it was inevitable that Justin and I would leave soon.

Morgan had just taken Victoria to bed and there would only be about ten others, all of whom would want to turn in before long. The thought of it made anticipation rush through me. My blood felt warm.

I had just been in the kitchen with some of my family, and I went to find Justin. He was standing across the room, talking to his parents who would be leaving on the last shuttle to the hotel. Some of the guests were staying in Seattle for a day or two, but some were going back right away—and Justin's parents were in that group. Their flight was scheduled to leave first thing in the morning, and we wouldn't see them again until their next trip.

I had only been separated from him for a short time, and yet it was a relief to see him. He was wearing a light blue suit with a white button-down shirt. The pants and jacket were made of a light linen material since it was summer, and all of the pieces were impeccably fitted, conforming to his broad-chested muscular body.

I had seen him without a shirt countless times, but I thought of him differently now that I had the option to really check him out. The evening was winding down, and found myself physically drawn to Justin—like I had no other choice but to cross to him. He saw me coming, and he smiled and stood back, making room for me in the group.

"Justin was just telling us you try to help tutor some of your students with their academics so they can get into better schools," his mom said.

"I do," I agreed. "I'm not great at math, but I can help them with most of what they need to do. Some of them don't get their work done if we don't do it at school, so I try to help as many as I can." I shrugged and smiled. "It feels like a drop in the bucket."

"Well, Justin said you like it and you're good at it. He said you might even keep doing it after you two start a family. Do you think you would?"

Justin's mother stared at me after she asked the question. I blinked. It was my first mother-in-law moment. She was asking me about future kids, and I didn't know what she wanted to hear as an answer. Honestly, I was so out-of-it that I wasn't even fully sure what she had asked.

"I'm sorry, I didn't hear you."

"Do you think you'll keep working once you have kids? Because with me in Oakland and your mom in Texas, I wasn't sure what you were thinking for childcare. You'll want to think about that if you work full-time."

She was smiling and speaking so quickly that it took a second for Justin to realize what she was saying and interject.

"Mom, Katie's, we're… we just got married today. We haven't talked about starting a family."

(We had, some, but this wasn't the time.)

"I can't say for sure how I'll feel when the time comes," I said. "I love my job, but I could see myself wanting to stay home, too."

"We'll figure it out," he assured her.

Justin pulled me in and put a protective arm around me. I leaned into him, feeling thankful for the steadying presence.

We spoke with his parents for the next five minutes while we waited on the shuttle. His mom asked me a few other things that could have put me on the spot, but I rolled with it, answering honestly and being myself. The whole party had been so unexpected that I had to be myself because I didn't have time to think of anything else.

And just like that, the second shuttle was pulling away. There were ten or twelve people at Mac's but they were spending the night at the house.

"When do I get to take you home?" Justin asked as we came back inside after seeing his parents off.

Everyone was across the room, and no one had heard him besides me.

I smiled at him and leaned against him as we walked. "I wish it was now, but reasonably, somewhere between sixteen and twenty-two minutes, probably."

"Eleven to sixteen," he said, countering my offer with one of his own.

I smiled at him.

"Fifteen," I said.

"Fifteen," he agreed.

We took a few steps toward the other side of the living room where others were sitting and standing.

"Ten," I said, getting lower.

"Eight," he countered.

"Five," I said, looking straight at him, daring him.

Justin stopped in his tracks, and because he was holding onto me, I had no choice but to do the same.

"Hey, everybody!" he said at full volume.

Every single person in the room looked our way.

"We're leaving." Justin was direct and unapologetic. "We'll see you all in the morning, maybe nine-thirty or ten. Nobody's leaving before then, right?" He didn't even give anyone time to answer before starting to walk backwards, pulling me with him. "Good. Love you all, and thank you for being here. We'll see you in the morning."

Justin waved at them before turning around and pulling me with him.

"Night!" I said, laughing a little.

"Goodnight and congratulations!" my mother yelled.

That sparked others to yell, too, and we walked out to a brief chorus of well wishes and cheers. That must've gotten Justin pumped because he was kissing me as soon as we rounded the corner. He stepped in front of me, walking backwards, intercepting me, kissing me, holding me, still walking.

I couldn't resist. I stopped walking and opened my mouth, letting him kiss me deeply, which he was more than ready to do. He stopped in the hallway, pushing me against the wall and kissing me like he thought we were at home alone. Several pulsing heartbeats passed where he kissed me so deeply I thought we might not make it home. I kissed him back because there was just no way I was going to pull away.

Finally, I did it. I broke contact.

"Juuus-tin," I said breathlessly.

"What?"

"We're still at Mac's," I whispered.

His chest shook with laughter. "I know."

"People are in here. We could get caught. We still have to walk across a hallway, a room, some steps and a porch, and then the driveway."

He laughed quietly again. "Thank you for the detailed description leading back to my apartment. I think I can find it now." He kissed me one more time before taking off, pulling me with him.

I was his wife now.

I was approaching the pinnacle of a really climatic day. Everything had been so unexpected that I felt somewhat taken off-guard that this moment was actually happening. I felt a slow, hot, heavy burn as I walked with Justin, following him, looking at his body.

We crossed the halls and rooms and driveways just like I said.

We came inside to decorations that our family had left out for us. There was music, rose petals, and the works.

It was nice of them and all, but Justin and I.... we were... we... hardly noticed.

Epilogue

Five months later
December

The Seahawks played and won on the 15th, and they weren't scheduled to play again for nine days. This meant we could squeeze in a trip home to Galveston to celebrate an early Christmas before Justin and Mac had to be back at work.

The guys were having a great season, and they were coming off of a win, so everyone was in the best mood when we went to Galveston. My family had always been big Seahawks fans on account of Mac, but they loved cheering for Justin, and they were fans of his since the moment he moved in with Mac.

Justin was a fun person to cheer for. He was a world-class, first-string, MVP player who was in a ton of offensive plays. I had always cared for Justin and been invested in his career, but now I was extremely protective, and for that reason, I hated what a rough sport football was.

I got more nervous than I used to. I was anxious for him every game and I had to do a lot of praying, for my own peace of mind.

Justin would say that my praying was the thing that made him know he loved me. I loved the Lord, but I definitely wouldn't think of myself as a good pray-er.

Justin's leg got dramatically better that night after I begged God to heal him, though. He tells that story, and tells everyone I have a direct line to God if they ever need anything.

We joked about it, but I could tell he thought I was more special than I was in that area, and his confidence in me made me try to get better, which was a nice side effect.

All this to say... Mac and Justin had fans who truly loved them in Galveston, and it was fun to go back home, not only as their loved one, Katie, but also as the girl who officially made Justin part of our family.

The trip was only for two nights, and we were on the second. We would leave in the morning, and Justin and Mac would be back at the field in Seattle for an afternoon practice.

Everyone, and I mean everyone, was at my parents' house for our family pre-Christmas-Christmas. The whole family was invited, and a lot of them brought guests who were close to our family as well. There were over a hundred people at my parents' house, and for two hours we shared a meal while listening to Christmas music and mingling with everyone.

It had been a long day of shopping, visiting, and preparing for the party. I was happy to see everyone, though and thankful for how much they loved Justin.

I hadn't been around him for the last hour. The men in my family took him to see something in my dad's shop, and he got stuck talking to a group of them. Justin found me right away when he came inside. He was wearing jeans and a white hoodie I bought for him. It looked amazing with his blue eyes. He came up behind me, pulling me into his arms and smelling my neck like he hadn't seen me in a long time.

"Your uncle is about to make his speech," he said, knowing the routine.

These kinds of speeches usually took several minutes. My Uncle Billy would speak, and then he we would go around and people would give quick updates—highlights from their individual families. It was really just a time to mention things we all knew since we were a close-knit family who kept each other informed throughout the year.

We would be settling in for a few minutes of talking, after which we would pile into a huge group and try to get a family picture that would, no doubt, turn out blurry since it was rushed and on someone's phone and there were a hundred of us. I knew these events would be taking place shortly.

There were so many people gathered into the two open rooms that Justin and I got by with hugging the outer edge and not being on anyone's radar.

At least I hoped that was the case. Because my husband was being mischievous. I had no idea what had gotten into him, but he stood behind me and held onto me in a tender way that caused me to feel a familiar rushing desire.

I leaned into him, turning my head, trying to get closer to his face. His cheek touched my ear, and then he kissed me, taking my earlobe gently into his mouth. He was barely out of view of about eighty people, and the feel of his warm breath on my ear made me feel weak in the knees.

My uncle Billy started talking, telling a story about a man in town who had bought a whole house because it came with one of Aunt Tess's paintings. He had mentioned it to us earlier tonight. I was glad I had heard it because there was no paying attention to what he was saying with my husband standing behind me like he was. Justin's mouth came close to my ear again, but before I could get my thoughts together enough to tell him he should wait, he whispered in my ear.

"He's about to say that I bought it, okay my love, just roll with it."

Just after Justin said that, Billy said something, and a round of gasps and cheers happened by my family. All of them turned to look at us. Justin's grip tightened and he held onto my waist. I glanced at him, and he smiled at everyone calmly before pulling back and focusing on me for a second and then back at everyone else. "My wife is learning about it for the first time right now," Justin said, smiling and holding onto me.

I looked straight at him. "What's going on?" I asked.

He grinned at me. "I bought that house," he said. "The story of the painting, that was me. I was going to give it to you for Christmas, I am giving it to you for Christmas. He just wanted to announce it."

Uncle Billy cut in, mediating and getting the family up-to-date on the current information.

"Justin and Katie live in Mac and Morgan's guesthouse. They said they were happy there and have plenty of room for now. So, instead of buying a house in Seattle, he bought that house here in Galveston. He and Katie will use it during the off-season."

"Thank you, Uncle Billy, for keeping me up-to-date on... my... life," I said in a stunned tone that made everyone laugh.

Uncle Billy said how proud they were of us before he went on with his speech, talking about two others who bought homes recently. "Nick bought a duplex and he's planning on living in one apartment and renting the other two—so if you know anybody looking for an apartment, talk to Nick. And also, Samuel bought a place back in November—a little house over on Jamaica Beach."

Everybody clapped for us, Nick, and Samuel, and Uncle Billy went on talking about how Mac and Morgan bought a new puppy for Victoria and she would be getting it when they got home.

I was glad they kept the conversation rolling, but I was stunned about the house. I knew exactly what house they were talking about when they told the story earlier. It was a historic place. Gorgeous. I thought the mayor lived there when I was a kid.

I stared at Justin like I couldn't believe any of this. "Thank you," I said. "I'm stunned. This seems like a moment where I should have something better to say than 'thank you' but gosh. Goodness." I smiled and regarded Justin, leaning into him. "Did you really buy that house?"

He nodded.

"The one with the palm trees?"

He nodded again.

I felt like the first lady of Galveston as I stood there with Justin—the first lady of the whole world.

"Are you happy?" he asked me, wondering if I liked the house.

I leaned back, molding my body to his, assuming the same position we were in before. I stretched up to speak to him and he gave me his ear so I could whisper in it. "The happiest," I said.

The End
(till book 9)

Thanks to my team ~ Chris, Coda, Jan, Glenda, and Yvette

Made in the USA
Middletown, DE
04 December 2021

54286986R00118